T

There was absolutely no reason why Dee Lawrence's and Nat Archer's paths should cross—but somehow they did, to Dee's dismay and fury. For every time they met the sparks flew—and what was far worse, Nat always got the better of her. Why didn't he just *go away*?

Books you will enjoy
by SUE PETERS

MARRIAGE IN HASTE
Trapped in a Far Eastern country on the brink of civil war, Netta could only manage to escape if she married Joss de Courcy—a man she knew only by his reputation, as 'The Fox'. She didn't have much choice in the circumstances—but did he have to treat her as *quite* such a helpless idiot?

CLAWS OF A WILDCAT
'I travel alone. I can't be bothered with encumbrances—however attractive,' Dominic Orr had told Margaret uncompromisingly. But after all, she was a career girl too; her job as a doctor was just as important to her as his as a geologist on an oil rig was to him. So where was the problem?

SHADOW OF AN EAGLE
Why had Marion taken such an immediate and instinctive dislike to Reeve Harland when he turned up to stay in her peaceful valley home? It was almost as if she had some premonition of what he was there for. Yet she didn't know, for quite a long time—and by then it was too late...

THE STAYING GUEST
Laura had hated having to turn her beloved home into a hotel, but she hadn't had any choice if she wanted to keep the place at all—and at least there was a certain interest in involving herself with all the varied personal problems of her guests. Until Martin Deering arrived, and Laura couldn't think about anyone's problems but her own!

TUG OF WAR

BY
SUE PETERS

MILLS & BOON LIMITED
15-16 BROOK'S MEWS
LONDON W1A 1DR

All the characters in this book have no existence outside the imagination of the Author, and have no relation whatsoever to anyone bearing the same name or names. They are not even distantly inspired by any individual known or unknown to the Author, and all the incidents are pure invention.

The text of this publication or any part thereof may not be reproduced or transmitted in any form or by any means, electronic or mechanical, including photocopying, recording, storage in an information retrieval system, or otherwise, without the written permission of the publisher.

This book is sold subject to the condition that it shall not, by way of trade or otherwise, be lent, resold, hired out or otherwise circulated without the prior consent of the publisher in any form of binding or cover other than that in which it is published and without a similar condition including this condition being imposed on the subsequent purchaser.

First published 1981
Australian copyright 1981
Philippine copyright 1981
This edition 1981

© Sue Peters 1981

ISBN 0 263 73472 2

Set in Monophoto 10 on 11 pt Baskerville

Made and printed in Great Britain by
Richard Clay (The Chaucer Press), Ltd., Bungay, Suffolk

CHAPTER ONE

'Stop! Don't go! Hi there, wait a minute....'

What *did* you have to shout, Dee wondered furiously, to prevent the driver of a red pick-up truck from disappearing with your suitcase full of unmentionables in the back of his vehicle? What was worse, she gulped unhappily, they were somebody else's unmentionables. It would not have been so bad if they were her own.

'Thank goodness, he's heard me!'

Through the open driving window, she could see the man's head turn in her direction as he swung his vehicle across the small station forecourt. Dee waved her arm at him, and started to run towards the van. She could see black wavy hair and a lean, darkly tanned face framed in the window square, and—yes, she was not mistaken, she saw interestedly, the glint of a plain gold ear-ring in his right ear. She just had time to wonder if the opposite ear was adorned with its fellow, when a pair of eyes as black as the hair looked at her, through her, he craned his head forward to look round her as if she was a mere obstruction, she thought disbelievingly, and then, satisfied that the road to his right was clear, he swung the van on to the carriageway with an expert twist of the wheel, and without vouchsafing her a second glance he accelerated away from her along the road. In the process, his van wheel dissected a large puddle, and neatly transferred a goodly portion of muddy liquid from the road surface right across her stockings and shoes.

'Thief! Beast!'

The first was untrue. The driver was not aware that she had dumped her case in the back of his pick-up truck. And the second was unjust. He could not possibly know, since he did not deign to look back, that she was running too fast to avoid the spray from his wheels. But Dee was in no mood to be either truthful or just. She skidded to a halt on the soaking wet cobbles, and glared after the rapidly disappearing vehicle.

'E's gorn.'

The other half of the bus queue, a lady of mountainous proportions and a lugubrious expression, viewed her unsuccessful attempt to attract the driver's attention with a doleful interest.

'I can see that,' Dee retorted with asperity, then, 'What on earth shall I do?' she muttered worriedly. 'I suppose you don't know who he is?' she turned to the would-be bus passenger with sudden hope.

'Never seen 'im before.' Her hope was instantly quenched. 'I thought you knew 'im,' the laden traveller showed a capacity for observation. 'You put your case in the back of 'is truck,' she stated unarguably.

'I know, but that was because....' Dee bit her lip in frustrated exasperation. That was because of a whole series of minor misfortunes, she thought crossly. It had started that morning with her car engine. Which didn't.

'The wretched thing won't go.' She opened the bonnet and regarded the contents with a total lack of comprehension.

'Oh dear, that means I can't visit your uncle today.' Her aunt peered at the assorted bits of machinery with an ignorance equal to her own.

'Perhaps the garage people can help,' Dee offered swift comfort. It was impossible for her arthritic relative to make the long journey to the inland hospital by public transport. 'I'll phone them right away, they might come up with something.' She dialled, explained, listened, and her face fell.

'Not until this afternoon? But....' A disembodied male voice sounded as if it was trying to be helpful, and she slid her hand over the mouthpiece. 'Shall I order a taxi?' she hissed in an aside to her aunt, and the latter shook her head.

'They have such hard springs, I'd rather wait and go with you tomorrow. You can take your uncle's clean clothes and things, and bring back his washing,' she continued briskly when Dee put the receiver down on the promise that her car would be collected immediately after lunch.

'Why couldn't they have taken him to the local hospital?' she wondered, not for the first time. 'We could have taken the boat then, and gone along the river. You would have managed that easily enough.'

'It's only a cottage hospital in Penzyn,' her aunt replied philosophically. 'They haven't got the facilities for taking in a lot of patients at once, and there were sixteen people injured in the storm altogether, some of them quite badly.'

'Uncle Frank's got a broken hip,' Dee protested at the discrimination.

'Some of the others had broken heads,' her aunt said drily. 'But fortunately they're all on the mend now.'

'It must have been quite a storm.'

'It was. It was the worst this part of the coast has seen for many a year.' Martha Lawrence's faded eyes looked backwards into a past Dee could not share. 'Even your Uncle Frank can't remember a worse, in all the years he's been on the smacks,' she referred to the small fleet of inshore fishing boats which comprised her husband's business, one of which he still insisted on sailing himself, despite his sixty-five years.

'There's still a lot of evidence of the storm around Penzyn,' Dee remarked, 'they were shoring up part of the harbour wall the last time I was down there, as well as the jetties serving that big warehouse on the quay. The one belonging to whatsisname,' she said vaguely.

'The Archer quay,' her aunt nodded. 'I heard they'd taken quite a beating. But Wordesley Archer will cope, he's a fighter. He always was,' she added reminiscently.

'Wordesley Archer?' The name struck a chord with Dee. 'He and Uncle Frank are—sort of rivals—aren't they?' she enquired delicately. She had never understood the relationship between the two fleet owners. Their business interests did not clash, so it could not be that. Her uncle was in inshore fishing, and the Archer line were all cargo vessels. In such a small community it would seem normal for the two families to be friends, and yet the best that could be said of the only meeting she had ever witnessed between the two men was that they treated one another with a kind of wary respect, which pointed to what she sensed had been bitter antagonism when they were younger, which only age had managed to mellow. She had never bothered to question before, since her sojourns in the low stone house on the cliffs overlooking Penzyn had been for brief holiday visits only, which did not allow her time to form any lasting relationships with the local inhabitants. But since the consequences of the storm brought her hotfoot to the support of her only living relatives, the interchange of relationships in the small community had begun to involve herself, and so to intrigue her.

'Wordesley and Frank were rivals once,' her aunt smiled, and Dee stared at her, awakened to the fact that the tiny, white-haired figure leaning on her stick for support, had once been a lively golden-haired girl like herself, eagerly sought after by suitors.

'They *were* rivals, and Uncle Frank won?' she murmured intuitively.

'He won,' her aunt smiled contentedly. 'Now be off with you,' she changed the subject firmly. 'And don't forget to bring back your uncle's washing when you come home,' she called after Dee's retreating figure.

'That's it in the locker,' her uncle told her when she passed on her aunt's message some hours later. 'What they're still keeping me in here for I can't imagine,' he grumbled with the healthy discontent of a patient well on the road to recovery.

'They said you can come home just as soon as they take your plaster off,' Dee consoled.

'Plaster!' he growled. 'I'm boarded up like a box of fish.'

'You shouldn't grumble,' Dee rebuked him. 'You're being well looked after, and you said how good the food is.'

'Oh, I'm being looked after fine. These lassies do a grand job,' he nodded approval to a bright-faced passing nurse. 'And the food's not bad, in its way, apart from the fish. Do you know,' he heaved himself up in bed to emphasise his point, 'last Friday they asked me if I'd like fish. And there was I, looking forward to a tasty bit of cod, and when it turned up it was fish fingers. *Fish fingers!*' he repeated incredulously. 'And for all the taste there was to it, it might as well have been the cardboard box it came wrapped up in.' He spoke with the disgust of a man accustomed to eating fish fresh caught from the sea.

'You're some way inland here,' Dee laughed aloud at his expression. 'You can't expect the hospital to get fish fresh from the boats, the same as we do.'

'They will in future,' her uncle declared. 'The moment they let me out of this straitjacket, I've promised to send them a fresh supply every Friday from now on. Fish fingers!' he snorted disgustedly.

Dee hid her smile in the suitcase as she dutifully sorted out the clean pyjamas, homely striped wincyette and no nonsense about them. It was a typically kindly gesture on the part of the veteran fisherman, she thought, and she was still smiling as she came out of the station and headed for the nearby bus stop for the last lap of her journey home. Her smile faded as she studied the timetable.

'It's gorn.' It seemed to be the mountainous woman's favourite expression.

'I thought it was supposed to coincide with the train times?'

'The train was late.'

'Only by a minute or two.' But the bus driver had not waited.

'I wish I hadn't brought a white suitcase.' Dee had not given her choice a thought when she started out from home under clear skies. She simply grabbed the nearest case of handy size from the hall closet. It was one of her own, with which she had travelled down, but now, grimacing at the steady downpour which greeted her as she emerged into the station yard, she regretted her choice.

'The next bus'll be forty minutes.'

Dee looked from her informant to the empty station yard with growing dismay. Rain dripped with depressing persistence, running muddy rivulets in between the cobbles. She shivered. The wetness made it cold, and the nearest thing that offered comfort was a mechanical drinks dispenser at the other end of the forecourt. She looked round for somewhere to rest her case. She could not struggle with case, handbag, coins and a plastic beaker of hot liquid all at the same time, but no handy flat surface presented itself, and the rain, and the unsoiled whiteness of her case, denied her the easy way out of simply putting it down on the ground.

'May I leave it in the station office until the bus comes?' It was not heavy, but she did not relish holding it for another forty minutes. Its light weight made it a plaything for the brisk breeze which whipped across the open space and banged the case against her legs with irritating persistence. The uniformed figure appearing at the station entrance seemed to offer a solution.

'Sorry, miss,' he promptly removed her newborn hope. He did not look particularly sorry, Dee thought crossly, and controlled her irritation with difficulty. The day had gone badly enough as it was, without having a row with a station porter.

'But surely——,' she began to protest.

'We're closing the station, miss,' the man explained with the weary patience of one who has said the same thing, dozens of times before, to passengers who never seemed to listen. 'There won't be another train now until after five o'clock, and as it's only a halt, and not a proper station, it isn't worth keeping it open if there's no passengers,' he pointed out reasonably. 'You can leave your case and come back for it after five o'clock, if you like.' He tried his best to be helpful.

'I'm catching the next bus.' Dee shook her head.

'Ah well, in that case you've not got long to wait. It's only forty minutes.'

Only forty minutes! With an effort, Dee checked a surge of impatience. The sheer slowness of life in Penzyn and its surrounds had to be experienced to be believed, she marvelled. She had enjoyed it at first, after the busy life of a commercial laboratory it was pleasantly relaxing to have time to stand and stare, but now, although she was careful not to let it show in front of her elderly relatives, she found it was beginning to irk her.

'I'll have to put up with it until Uncle Frank's on his feet again,' she told herself for the umpteenth time. 'It'd be mean to leave Aunt Martha on her own, she can't drive herself so she'd be housebound without me. It isn't as if I've got to worry about getting back to my job.' She frowned. The thought of her job irked her even more than the slowness of life in Penzyn.

'I've left the firm,' she had told her aunt stormily, explaining her ability to act as a companion to her delighted relative when the news of her uncle's injury first brought her to the coast. 'The firm's been taken over by one of those big multi-national companies, and they've built some super new laboratories. And put a *man* in charge of them,' she added disgustedly. 'Would you believe, they asked me to be his assistant!' She choked on the indignity of the offer.

'Perhaps they thought you were a bit young to be in charge,' her aunt placated.

'I don't see why,' Dee argued. 'I've had my own lab at Grimleys for over a year now. Oh, the man they've put in charge of the new lab is a lot older than me,' she acknowledged. 'He must be at least forty.' Her aunt's lips twitched, but Dee was too angry to notice. 'He doesn't have any better qualifications than I've got. No, he got the job simply because he's a man,' she fumed. 'Sometimes I hate men!' she declared bitterly. 'They talk about equality, but they only pay lip service to it.'

'Perhaps your new job will give you more scope,' her aunt suggested tactfully.

'I don't start there until the autumn, when their present chemist retires,' Dee answered. Which meant she would have to adjust her pace to that of Penzyn for another several weeks.

She looked round the station yard, seeking inspiration. Faced with a long wait, the rain seemed colder than ever, and the drinks dispenser proved irresistible. Except that she was still hampered by the suitcase. Her eyes lit on a small red pick-up truck parked near to the station entrance. There was no sign of the driver, and no lettering on the outside of the truck to indicate to whom it belonged. She peeped inside the back load-space. It was sheltered by a tonneau cover, and although the back number plate was almost obliterated by mud, the inside load-space seemed to be clean and dry. On an impulse she lifted her case into the truck and tucked the cover round it for protection.

'The driver won't mind, just for a minute or two,' she assured herself. The drinks dispenser was only a few yards away, and she would surely hear if the van driver came back and started his engine.

She did not bargain for the prolonged, high-pitched

buzz emitted by the drinks dispenser. It whined like a banshee, and too late she became aware that the bang she heard must be the van driver slamming his door shut, preparatory to starting away. The van began to move across the station yard even as she turned.

'Stop! Don't go! Hi, there, wait a minute....'

All that she got for her pains was a pair of soaking wet legs and feet.

'I hope a traffic warden notices his filthy number plate, and pulls him up,' she wished uncharitably, and even as she wished, she knew that it was impossible. Traffic wardens were as yet an unknown addition to the local forces of law and order, and the most that was likely to happen to the driver was that the local constable might provide a bucket of water and a brush for him to sluice his number plate clean, in case he should meet up with a 'foreign' Panda car from over the border into the next county. A kindly gesture that, applied to herself, she would have taken to be no more than reasonable, but applied to the villain who was making off with her case, she would regard as a gross dereliction of duty, she thought wrathfully.

'You'll miss the bus if you don't come.'

It trundled into the yard and forced her to leave her hot drink behind. Not that it mattered now, she thought crossly, rising temper did all the warming that was necessary, and it did not help when she boarded the rattly vehicle that there was only one vacant seat left, and the mountainous woman with her numerous bundles elected to take the portion next to the window, leaving Dee with about two inches of the edge on which to find precarious rest for the remainder of the way home.

She squirmed and twisted in a vain attempt to get comfortable, and eventually gave up the effort as the bus reached the outskirts of Penzyn and pointed its nose along the narrow main street which split the town neatly in two. Penzyn was built on a long, narrow peninsula, and was effectively divided into what the inhabitants called its 'bread' and 'jam' halves. The 'bread' half comprised the deep natural harbour which sheltered the working boats. The inshore fishing fleet, a large part of which belonged to her uncle, and the cargo vessels, the bulk of which were made up by Wordesley Archer's fleet. The 'jam' half of the town was on the opposite side of the peninsula, that enjoyed a broad sandy beach and shallower water, and attracted a goodly crowd of holidaymakers each summer, providing a pleasant livelihood for the scatter of small hotels that lined the promenade.

'Ooh, my back feels as if it's breaking!' Dee gained the pavement with a sigh of relief. 'I'd rather walk the rest of the way than endure another minute of that awful seat,' she groaned. It was a good two miles still to her aunt's house, but the walk was preferable to riding in such conditions. 'Besides, my car might be ready by now.' She brightened. 'It's worth dropping in at the garage to ask.' It was a forlorn hope, but it was better than nothing, and the delay in returning home would give her time to think up an explanation of how she had come to virtually give away two brand new pairs of wincyette pyjamas, to say nothing of sundry other odds and ends which had been placed in her safe keeping, one of which, she remembered guiltily, was an expensive electric razor which she had exhanged that afternoon for one of a battery type, which her uncle said would be more convenient to use while he was confined to bed.

'Sorry, Miss Lawrence, your car won't be ready today. In fact, it may not be usable for a couple of days yet,' the garage foreman dashed her hopes, and spoke with the gloomy inevitability of a dentist telling a patient, 'I'm afraid it'll have to come out. . . .'

'It's a touch of carburettor trouble. That's the difficulty when these twin carb jobs go wrong.' He rubbed his hands on a rag as oily as his fingers, and continued to blind Dee with science. 'If you get an imbalance between the carbs it can take a while to get it running sweetly again. They're very delicately balanced, you know.' She did not, but she tried to look intelligent about it, while thrusting down an unpleasant feeling that her informant was only too well aware of her abysmal ignorance, and happily making capital out of it. Her own unselfconscious lack of vanity did not suspect that her petite figure, topped by a shoulder-length bob of deep gold hair with intriguing copper lights in it, and appealing navy blue eyes, might have something to do with his obvious desire to keep her talking. 'It has to be tested, then adjusted and tested again.' He seemed prepared to go on indefinitely.

'Perhaps you'll ring me when it's ready?' Dee began to get restless. She still had a two-mile walk home, and she would much rather the garage man occupied himself with her car engine than with explaining incomprehensible mechanical details.

'Come into the office for a minute, and give me your phone number.'

Surely he must know her uncle's number? she thought irritably, but, unwilling to antagonise an expert on carburettors, she followed him meekly through a door into a cluttered room made claustrophobic by volumes of paperwork, askew calendars, mysterious spare bits of mechanical equipment in odd boxes, and——

'You!'

He only wore an ear-ring in his one ear, she observed confusedly. His right ear. The one she had seen through the open driving window of the red pick-up truck. His left ear was unadorned. He removed himself casually from the edge of the cluttered desk, and stood up as they came through the door. He seemed to fill the room. Dee had to tip her head back to look up at him, and she did not take kindly to the glint of laughter that lurked in the depths of the black eyes that surveyed her interestedly from much too far above her head. They seemed to mesmerise her. With an effort she dragged her own eyes away, and saw for the first time what his move from the desk had revealed.

'My case!' It resided on the sole, and rickety, office chair. She reached out towards it eagerly.

'*Your* case?' He put a detaining hand on the handle, and his emphasis held an insulting question.

'Of course it's mine,' she flared angrily. 'I put it in the back of your truck while....'

'You did?' He did not remove his hand from the handle, and short of an undignified struggle, which Dee had a nasty feeling she would lose anyway, there was no way to wrest her property from him. 'Can you describe the contents?' he asked her smoothly. The laughter transferred itself from his eyes to curve his well cut lips, and Dee's temper flared. After a day of constant obstacles, to have this overbearing stranger doubt her word over a mere suitcase was too much. She snapped,

'Of course I can describe them. They're....' She became aware of the foreman's interested presence, and her colour rose. 'They're—er—nightclothes and—er—toilet articles.' She had not the slightest intention, she told herself crossly, of giving details of her uncle's homely nightwear and equipment for the amusement of the two men, particularly the black-haired one. He said,

'We'd better check the contents, just to make sure. It's a nice case, but....' He eyed it critically.

It was a beautiful case. It bore the hallmark of an exclusive brand, and was one of a set of luggage which had been donated to her by her ex colleagues as a leaving gift.

'....but there must be thousands like it,' he continued smoothly, 'so we've got to be sure it's the one you—er—say belongs to you.'

Again the implied doubt. Her cheeks flamed. She had an urge to pick up her case and bring it down—hard—on top of his arrogant head. With a great effort she controlled herself, and said icily,

'My address is on the label inside the case. My name's Lawrence. . . .'

'I can vouch for who you are, Miss Lawrence,' the foreman butted in helpfully, and turned to the other man. 'This lady's living with her relatives up at Cliff House.' Although it had never been officially named, everyone locally called her uncle's home Cliff House, and Dee blessed the foreman's intervention. It was just what was needed, she thought with malicious satisfaction, to put this interfering stranger firmly in his place.

'*Dee* Lawrence?' He flicked open the case lid without even a by your leave, she thought vexedly, resenting his intrusion into the privacy of her luggage.

'Feel free,' she told him sarcastically.

'I do,' he replied imperturbably. 'The case appeared out of nowhere in the back of my truck, and until I find its rightful owner. . . .'

'I *am* its rightful owner. I only left it in your truck while I went to the drinks machine at the station, because I couldn't leave it on the cobbles in the wet.'

'Hmmm,' he said noncommittally, and gave her a level look. 'Dee. It could be a man's name, as well as a woman's. And the address on the inside isn't Cliff House,' he observed shrewdly. 'It says,' he read, 'Flat 3, Grosvenor Court. . . .'

'I'm in Penzyn on a prolonged visit,' Dee snapped, goaded out of her hard won calm by his effrontery. It was none of his business why she was here, and she was in no mood to give explanations to strangers. 'Normally I live in a flat convenient to my job,' she finished abruptly. Convenient to what had been her job, but she had no intention of enlarging on that, either.

'How emancipated,' he murmured, and her lips tightened, but before she could say anything he went on interestedly, 'It's either a man's suitcase, or you've taken this equality business to heart.' To her chagrin he reached into the case and picked out a pair of the striped wincyette pyjama trousers between a critical forefinger and thumb, and held them up to view. 'They seem a bit on the large side for you.' His eyebrows raised, and his black, laughing eyes—she felt a strong urge to box his ears—his eyes roamed boldly over her dainty figure, around which the offending pyjama trousers would wrap at least twice, and still have room to spare.

'P-p-put those down!' she ordered him wrathfully, total embarrassment making her stammer. She could feel the foreman's broad grin behind her back, and her face went scarlet with mortification. She felt as if she was blushing all over, she thought furiously, right down to the tips of her toes. She grabbed at the trousers with trembling fingers, and disconcertingly he released them without a struggle, but only in order to pick up the electric razor. 'A man's shaver, too,' he observed, and inspected the implement approvingly. 'It's an excellent make, I couldn't have chosen better myself.'

'Oh, do stop fooling!' Without warning the frustrations of the day caught up with Dee, and she felt a sudden humiliating desire to cry. 'All this belongs to my uncle.' Her voice came out flat and lifeless, and with a tremble in it she could not control. 'I'm bringing back his washing from the hospital.' She choked to a halt, furious with herself for her untimely lack of control.

'How is your uncle, Miss Lawrence?' The foreman's face lost its grin, and looked sympathetic. She did not know if the stranger's face had lost its grin as well, she did not turn to look. She did not dare, in case he should see the sudden over-brightness of her eyes. 'How's Mr Lawrence going along?' the foreman enquired. 'I heard he'd taken quite a toss in that storm we had a few weeks back.'

'He's getting along fine.' Everyday courtesies came to the rescue of her swiftly vanishing poise, and her voice lost its tremble as she went on, 'With luck we may have him home within a week or two.'

'I won't keep you waiting for your car any longer than I

can help,' the garage man promised kindly. 'You'll need it for visiting him. I don't suppose your aunt can manage to travel on public transport, not with her having arthritis and all.'

'No, it was a big disappointment to them both that she couldn't go today,' Dee confessed. 'She'll be waiting for me to get home and tell her how he is.' In control of herself again, she terminated the conversation firmly, and turned to reach for her case.

'I'd like to give you a lift back home,' the foreman said considerately. 'It's a long way to Cliff House, and mostly uphill, and you carrying your case all the way.' At least the foreman acknowledged her right to her case, she thought with relief, and could not resist a small, triumphant glance at the stranger. She looked away again hastily. His eyes were resting on her, as if he had been watching her all the time. 'The trouble is,' the foreman continued, 'the two mechanics are both out on test for the next hour, and I daren't leave the garage unattended until they come back.'

'I'll enjoy the walk,' Dee lied robustly. She would not. Quite suddenly, she felt extremely weary. It was probably the effects of temper, she acknowledged honestly. The black-haired stranger seemed to have the power to bring out the very worst in her, and she bitterly regretted having compromised herself by making free with his truck. It would have been far less trouble to wash mud-stains from her case.

Without bothering to look round—to do so would have meant facing the dark-eyed stranger again, and she felt a curious reluctance to do so—she reached back to grasp the handle of her case. Her fingers groped, found, and closed, and she found herself grasping a set of long, slim fingers which still rested firmly across the case handle. She snatched her hand away as if she had been stung, and coloured furiously.

'Give me. . . .' Her eyes snapped.

'Certainly,' he answered agreeably. 'When we reach Cliff House,' he added firmly.

'When *we* reach...?' She ground to an uncertain halt. What did he mean—we? 'I'm not going anywhere with you,' she declared forthrightly.

'On the contrary,' he contradicted her cheerfully, 'you're going to accept a lift in my truck, along with your case, as far as Cliff House.' So he acknowledged it was her case now. Strangely, the realisation gave her no satisfaction. Faced with this other, more immediate dilemma, it did not seem important.

'It'll save you a fair walk, Miss Lawrence,' the foreman urged, clearly relieved that the other man echoed his own good intentions. 'And it won't be all that much out of Mr Archer's way.'

'Archer? Did you say—Archer?' Dee lost any appreciation she might have had of good intentions, and her startled mind focussed on one word only.

'The youngest of the Archer line, at your service.' The black-haired man sketched a mocking bow.

'Nonsense!' Dee told him coldly. 'Wordesley Archer only has two sons.' She had seen them—Charles and William. They were both much older than the stranger, and so very different. She tried not to let herself think that the difference was to the former's disadvantage. Charles and William, as their names implied, were solid, worthy men, partners in their father's shipping business. And about as exciting as their own cargo vessels, a small imp inside her suggested. They were both married to serious, worthy women, and no doubt their offspring dutifully took after their parents. How dull! the imp mourned, unrepentantly.

'My worthy half-brothers.' She looked up, startled. How did he manage to read her thoughts so accurately? Perhaps they simply reflected his own....

'Nathan, here, isn't at home all that much,' the foreman indicated their mutual companion. 'And you coming only on short visits until now, I don't expect you've bumped into one another before.' He made what passed for an introduction.

It was a happy omission, Dee thought sourly, but for the foreman's sake she did not say so out loud. He was not to know that the Archer family were a subject not much discussed at Cliff House, which would explain why she had never heard the third son mentioned. He said 'half-brothers', which told her that Wordesley Archer must have married for a second time. Judging by the age of the black-haired man, she studied him more carefully and came to the conclusion that he must be about twenty-eight or nine to her own twenty-five years, she reckoned that Wordesley Archer's second wife had been considerably younger than himself.

The only time she had met the other Archer men was once at a civic function, to which the two fleet owners and their families had been invited, and being on holiday at Cliff House at the time, she had accompanied her aunt and uncle to the formal affair, which she was sure Charles and William had enjoyed, but she most certainly did not. Her uncle, sharing her feelings, put it in a nutshell.

'Thank goodness it only comes once a year!'

Nathan Archer looked as if he might be of the same mind as herself about such functions, she deduced. But that still did not make it a good idea for her to accept a lift from him, even if she wanted to. Which she most certainly did not. With the strained feeling between the heads of the two families, it was patently impossible for her to allow him to accompany her to Cliff House. Common courtesy would oblige her to ask him in, and.... Her mind boggled at the thought of her aunt's possible reaction. It went a paralysed blank at the possibility of what her fiery uncle might say to such an invasion. To make matters even worse,

'I'm the black sheep of the family,' Nathan Archer confessed gravely, and without shame.

CHAPTER TWO

'They've altered the road system since I was home last,' Nathan Archer conversed easily as he drove.

'It's two years since it was finished,' Dee answered him shortly.

'It's three since I was home,' he replied laconically, and added, 'There's a fork in the road coming up. Which way do we go, right or left?'

'Right,' Dee answered automatically, and wondered why she was sitting next to Nathan Archer in the red pick-up truck, riding towards Cliff House with him as if it was the most natural thing in the world for her to do.

'How on earth did I come to agree to ride with him?' she asked herself for the hundredth time. When he suggested—no, told—her to come with him, she said 'No!' forcefully, and meant it, and with a shrug he picked up her case and made off with it towards the truck, and it was either follow him, or lose sight of her case again. And so she followed him, angrily, reluctantly, but she still followed, because she had no option, and now she was sitting beside him with her property in her lap, wondering how to explain his presence to her aunt when they eventually reached Cliff House.

'I won't ask him in, then they needn't meet,' she settled the problem decidedly.

'I should have known better,' she acknowledged resignedly, ten minutes later. The day looked like finishing as badly as it had started. The brisk breeze had chased the clouds inland and the sun was already beginning to dry the road surface. Why could it not have shone earlier? she wondered crossly. If it had, she would not be in this difficulty now.

But it hadn't, and she was. And what was more, the sun had tempted her aunt to walk as far as the garden gate to watch for her coming. She was accompanied as usual by Skip, the wirehaired terrier. As they pulled up at the gateway Dee could hear the lively little animal engaged in its favourite occupation of barking at the circling gulls.

'Don't-bother-I'll-get-myself-out-thank-you-for-the-lift-goodbye,' Dee gabbled all in one long, hasty sentence, and turned quickly to open the passenger door for herself almost before the truck wheels had stopped turning. 'It's locked,' she discovered angrily, and spun round on him with an accusing glare.

'It's only stuck,' he contradicted her mildly. 'That's why I went to the garage, to see if they could order me a new lock, because this one jams.' He opened his own door with a leisurely hand. 'Sit still,' he bade her, unnecessarily, since without his help she was unable to get out of the truck anyhow, 'I'll have to open the door from the outside.'

'He must have known it would stick when he shut me in,' she muttered angrily, and glared through the windscreen as his lithe figure rounded the bonnet, and he strolled unhurriedly to her own side of the car, nodding across to her aunt on the way, she saw uneasily. So much for her determination that the two should not meet! He reached down and fiddled with the door handle. There was an anguished mechanical sound from somewhere inside, and he gave the handle a hefty wrench. The door opened a crack, and Dee did not wait for him to pull it ajar. She swung her legs out of the passenger well, and leaned sideways to give the door a push, just as Nathan Archer pulled, and the sudden cessation of resistance ejected her through the gap with a velocity that landed herself and her case in a crumpled and humiliating heap at his feet.

'Not so fast,' he chided, and bending he scooped her up and stood her on her feet again, then, still holding her arm, leaned over and began to brush her down with his other hand. 'I say,' his eyes took in her mud-splashed stockings and shoes, and he paused in his ministrations. 'You're in quite a state! No wonder you didn't want to put your case down on the station cobbles, if it was that muddy.' To her intense relief, he made no attempt to brush her stockings.

'I'll box his ears if he does,' she fumed inwardly, and aloud she hissed, 'It's your fault I'm in this state in the first place! Your truck wheel went through a muddy puddle, and this is the result,' she snapped.

He did not look in the least repentant, she thought angrily, and he took not the slightest notice of her plea. His hand remained where it was, his slim brown fingers grasping her arm with a firm hold that, without actually using force, she could not break away from. She moved restlessly.

'For goodness' sake, loose me!' She felt suddenly, unaccountably disturbed by his touch, and a thrill akin to fear ran through her, and sharpened her voice as she added, 'And stop looking at my....' She nearly said 'legs,' blushed, swallowed, and said 'stockings,' instead, and saw from the ready laughter that lit his black eyes that he guessed at her hasty amendment, and mocked her for it.

'They're pretty—er—stockings, underneath the mud splashes,' he drawled. He loosed her, then, and she drew in a sharp breath that could have been relief or it could have been disappointment. Her arms tingled from where his hands had held her, and she bent hurriedly to pick up her case, with a strange feeling of being bereft as he turned away from her and said courteously to her aunt at the gate,

'I gave Dee a lift home from Penzyn.'

'Cheek!' she muttered angrily at his free use of her Christian name. She had not given him permission to....

'You're Nathan Archer, aren't you? The one they call Nat?' To Dee's utter astonishment, her aunt smiled up at the self-acknowledged black sheep of the Archer clan, and went on calmly in her soft voice, 'You were nothing but a leggy boy the last time I saw you.'

He was far from being a leggy boy now, Dee thought caustically. He was tall, with a man's straight, confident carriage; slim, with a man's lean, muscular strength. The sleeves of his black sweater, casually pushed up to the elbows, revealed hard brown arms well capable of a man's work. But he did not seem to mind her aunt's reference. He smiled across at the white-haired woman as if she was his own relative, Dee thought in amazement.

'I give up!' she shrugged helplessly. The whole day had been topsy-turvy, and now her aunt was confounding all her preconceived fears by actually being nice to the youngest Archer.

'And why not?' reason asked her. Because, years ago, Wordesley Archer had loved and lost, it did not necessarily make Martha hate him, even if the relationship between her husband and his ex-rival was the reverse of cordial.

'I went to see if my car was ready,' Dee interrupted abruptly. 'Nat was at the garage at the same time as me,' she deliberately retaliated by using the shortened, familiar version of his own name, and saw him slant a quick glance towards her, but she looked away and ignored it. His name sounded like something with a sting, she thought maliciously, and tried to stifle the feeling that the touch of his hands on her arms *had* left a sting behind them. They throbbed still, where he had held her, the more so because he no longer did. . . . 'The car may be a day or two before it's ready, the garage foreman said it was carburettor trouble.' She spoke urgently, afraid of the trend of her own thoughts.

'Oh dear!' Her aunt's face fell. 'That means I shan't be able to visit your uncle. He's at St Christopher's,' she explained to Nat Archer, mentioning the hospital in the county town.

'That needn't be a problem,' he responded readily. 'I've got to go and see Wainwrights, the ship's brokers, tomorrow. Their offices aren't far from the hospital, and I could easily drop you there, and pick you up when you're ready to come home,' he offered.

'No,' Dee instantly refused. It was unthinkable that they should be under an obligation to Nathan Archer.

'How kind,' her aunt cut across what she was about to say. She did not seem to hear her, and yet normally her hearing was acute enough. Dee looked at her suspiciously. Perhaps her desire to see her husband had overridden her normal sturdy independence. 'Will two o'clock be all right?' she asked Nat sweetly.

'I might as well be invisible,' Dee thought vexedly, as the two made their plans for the next day without any reference to herself.

'At least they won't expect me to go with them,' she thought with relief.

There was only one passenger seat in the pick-up truck. She bent down and made a pretence of fussing the terrier, and deliberately did not respond to Nat's cheerful wave as he jackknifed his long length back into the truck, and reversing in a single skilful sweep, left them to walk back to the house on their own.

'What does he want at Wainwrights, I wonder? What does he do, anyway?' Curiosity overcame Dee's reluctance to ask questions. Wainwrights, she knew, were ship's brokers specialising in handling the purchase and sale of vessels.

'Surely you've heard of Nathan Archer?' Her aunt viewed her across the tea cups with unfeigned surprise. 'Author, photographer—I thought you enjoyed reading travel books? They're making his latest series into a film.'

'*That* Nathan Archer,' Dee exclaimed. 'No wonder his name sounded familiar, and not just because of the Archer shipping line, either.' She had not given the connection a thought until now. The monogram on his book jackets was familiar, too, she realised. The encircled figure of an archer that graced the spines of his books was a replica of the bow badges she had seen carried by the family's cargo vessels. Not the Cupid kind of archer, she remembered with a sudden upcurving of her lips, but the kneeling figure of a hunter, intent on speeding his arrow in silent flight towards who knew what unsuspecting prey? Impulsively she curled her fingers round her cup, childishly seeking comfort from its warmth. Unreasonably she felt herself to be vulnerable, and a little afraid, though she could not explain what she was afraid of, even to herself.

'The backgrounds of his books are diverse enough,' she admitted grudgingly. 'I wonder how he manages to get the feel of them so accurately?' Even in his works of fiction, his backgrounds were those of a man who knew them, because he had lived them, and his photography displayed brilliance lifted into another world by a sensitive artistry that achieved breathtaking results. His subjects ranged from the Arctic to the Azores. 'His range is practically world-wide,' she tempted her aunt to talk, without actually questioning her, and despised herself for doing so. She did not want to know about Nat Archer, she did not like the man, she told herself fiercely, but something inside her for which she could not account drove her to find out about him just the same.

'He's worked an ocean-going tug for the last three years,' her aunt replied obligingly. She seemed to know a good deal about him, Dee thought, and then remembered that her aunt was a member of the local Women's Guild, from whose meetings she always returned primed with all the neighbourhood news. 'It's given him all the background he's needed for his books, and an interesting occupation at the same time.'

'There's an ocean-going tug tied up in the harbour,' Dee remembered. 'I noticed it when I was down there last week. It was huge.' The vessel was a far cry from the small tugs she was used to, that scudded to and fro like water beetles, ferrying barges loaded with freight, and coping with the myriad jobs that were necessary in the small but busy harbour. Because of its size she had noticed the big tug particularly, but she assumed it to be a bird of passage, wafted into the harbour like a migrant off course, forced in, perhaps, by the need to make an emergency repair.

'The work the ocean-going tugs have to do is huge,' her aunt commented, with the casual acceptance of a woman of the coast, accustomed to the needs of shipping men. 'They tow the big oil tankers into berth, and cope with deep-water salvage and fire-fighting work. They've even been known to tow an iceberg out of the way of the shipping lanes.'

'That was in one of his books. Towing an iceberg, I mean.' A strange excitement coursed through Dee, and refused to be subdued.

'I wonder if he used the *Sea Wind* for that particular job?' The name of the vessel had stuck in her memory, caught at her imagination. It epitomised the world of the big tug, free-ranging across the oceans, ready to answer the call to work in any climate, under any conditions, from the Tropics to the Poles, braving seas that lesser ships would not dare. That was the difference between Nat Archer and his half-brothers, she sensed intuitively. The inner freedom that refused to be tied to a desk job, that demanded his artistic talent be given free rein. It was a man's work, a man's world. A world which he afterwards put into words, to awe his fellow men, and draw them, if only briefly, through the magic of his vivid writing, into a world they could not share.

Without warning, a cold sense of desolation settled on Dee, like the fog that on occasion blotted out the harbour, through which no light could be seen, and no sun shone. A man's world—she caught her breath in a sound that was not unlike a sob—a world in which a woman had no part.

He came punctually at two the next day, and he came in a car. A Rover, with ample room in it for five.

'I think Mrs Lawrence will be more comfortable in the front, with me.' Nat helped her into the car with punctilious care.

'And I'll be more comfortable in the back, without you,' Dee thought mutinously, but something in the look he gave her denied her the courage to say so out loud, and for the second time in two days she climbed into his vehicle against her will.

The moment the door shut behind her, she had an almost irresistible urge to fling it open again, and jump out—run away—do anything to put as much distance between herself and Nat Archer as was physically possible. But she knew with a desperate sureness that no matter how far she ran, she would not be able to escape his presence. It had invaded her dreams last night, ruined her appetite at breakfast this morning, so that most of her plate of good bacon and egg disappeared into Skip's willing jaws. She felt trapped, resentful. She sat tensed in the back seat of the car, her nails digging red marks into the palms of her hands, trying not to look, and yet finding her eyes continually drawn as if by a magnet, to the glint of the thin gold ear-ring resting neatly in the lobe of his right ear.

'My mother was superstitious. She gave me a talisman when I was a baby.' Briefly his fingers left the steering wheel and touched the ear-ring. Fingers with nails that were clean, cut short, and beautifully shaped, she noticed. 'I must say it seems to have worked.' His eyes laughed at her through the driving mirror, telling her he had been watching her—and knew she had been watching him. Taunting her. Inviting her to wonder what luck he believed his talisman had brought him? Was he referring to his work with his tug, or as a writer and photographer, or the fact that her aunt—or herself—were riding with him now in the car?

The lurking laughter deep in his eyes dared her to seek the answer. With an immense effort she wrenched her own eyes away and turned her face towards the car window, seeking diversion in the passing scenery. But Nat's face superimposed itself on the speeding countryside, and in desperation she shut her eyes to try and blot him out, only to find that he was still there behind her closed lids, so that in despair she opened them again, to discover that they were pulling up outside the hospital, and it was time to get out of the car, and contrarily now she did not want to.

'I'll pick you up just after five.' He seemed well primed with the extent of the visiting times, Dee thought grudgingly, and despised herself for the thrill of anticipation that made her eyes seek the parking lot the moment they emerged from the hospital doors when the visit was over.

'How was he?' Nat enquired politely as they started off, and Dee sat back with a sigh and allowed the conversation to wash over her. She made no attempt to join in, but all the time she was acutely aware of Nat. Of his deep, well modulated voice, questioning, commenting, answering, with an interest that could not possibly have been feigned. But, she noticed observantly, not once did he mention his own business with the ship's brokers. And she wondered. . . .

'Helen is taking me in tomorrow,' her aunt chatted on, mentioning a fellow member of her Guild, 'then we're going to have tea together. Oh, I mustn't forget,' she turned in her seat and appealed to Dee, 'one of the nurses in the ward is twenty-one tomorrow, and I'd like to take her a box of chocolates. A special one, with a picture on the front, and a ribbon.'

'You shall have it, as soon as we get back home,' Dee smiled indulgently. 'And if Helen's taking you to the hospital tomorrow, it'll give me a chance to get those shells I promised to give to the therapist,' she realised. 'I can go along the creek to the shell beach.' It was a beach that caught the flow of two converging currents, which seemed to bring shells of every description to rest among the pebbles, and for that reason was a happy hunting ground for locals and visitors alike. 'Apparently they encourage the people recovering from hand injuries to make jewel boxes, it helps to get their fingers working again, and the shells make an attractive decoration.'

It would also, she decided with relief, give her a much needed period of solitude in which to collect herself, and try and bring to order the conflicting mass of emotions that seemed to have taken control of her normally poised self since she had first set eyes on Nat Archer. Surely it was a lifetime ago, not just a brief twenty-four hours?

'We'll drop your aunt at Cliff House,' Nat spoke to Dee directly for the first time, forcing her to look at him. She refused to meet his eyes; her pulse did curious, uncomfortable things when she did. She concentrated instead on the tip of his ear, the one without the ear-ring, and remained stonily silent.

'I'll run you into Penzyn for the chocolates.'

'I'd rather walk,' she refused instantly.

'The shops will be shut by the time you get there, if you do,' her aunt protested. 'It's gone five o'clock now.'

'You'll ride with me,' Nat said decidedly, and Dee gritted her teeth and lapsed into seething silence as he pulled the car to a halt outside the gateway to Cliff House, and saw her aunt safely up the path and through the door, but not without first sending Dee a piercing look that told her she would regret any precipitate action to get out of the car while he was gone. When he returned he did not offer her the now vacant front seat beside him.

'I wouldn't have it if he did,' Dee told herself, but the omission, she was sure it was deliberate, rankled with an irritation that flared into angry speech as Nat swung the car into a left turn off the road, when Dee knew the way to the town centre lay straight on.

'You're going the wrong way,' she redirected him sharply.

'I want to call in at the harbour before we go on into town.' He did not ask her if she minded the delay, and she cast an ostentatious glance at her watch, but he either did not notice, or he chose to ignore the hint. Probably the latter, she decided wrathfully, and since the hands told her she still had twenty-five minutes before the shops closed, she could not justifiably protest, especially when he remarked as he got out of the car,

'I'll only be ten minutes. I want something from my cabin.'

He parked on the quayside close against where the big tug lay berthed. Dee looked up at it interestedly. She would have liked to see over the vessel, it intrigued her with its winches and water cannon and radar scanners, a complete sea-going jack of all trades, its whole appearance one of immense strength. But he did not suggest that she should accompany him, and she would die rather than ask, she told herself independently, and remained hunched in a corner of the back seat in the car, that for all its opulent luxury seemed suddenly bleak and bare.

If she turned her head she could see the bow badge on the tug from where she sat, the crouching figure of the archer neatly encircled, and seeming to point his arrow directly at her. She fidgeted uneasily and looked away, but against her will she found her eyes drawn back again to the bronze figure. Was it her imagination, or was his shaft aimed straight at the region of her heart?

'Don't be so silly!' Impulsively she flung open the car door and jumped out. A gang of stevedores was unloading one of the Archer cargo vessels further along the quay. A great loose net containing seven or eight enormous sacks of something or other was being swung by crane from ship to shore. 'I'll go and watch, it'll pass the time,' she decided. It would also, she thought with satisfaction, show Nat that she was not prepared to sit meekly in the car, and await the time when he should condescend to return. And if he did not return soon, she glanced at her watch with a frown, it would be too late to obtain the chocolates anyway. As it was, they would have to stop at the first shop they came to, and risk getting the picture box which her aunt wanted. She could only spare a couple of minutes or so herself, to watch the unloading, then she would have to return to the car.

The net of sacks was being loaded on to pallets, she saw, and then stacked on a lorry. A pile of empty pallets waiting to be used stood between herself and the stevedores whom she could hear talking beside the lorry. The pile effectively blocked her view of what was happening as the crane swung the net of heavy sacks in an arc high across her, across the stack of empty pallets, to drop down on the other side for the men, still invisible to her, to empty the net and return it for another load. The sacks contained some kind of white powder. A snowy trickle descended from one of them now being swung in the net towards her, across the ship's side.

'I wonder what it is?' Curiosity compelled her to hold out her hand palm upwards. In another minute the load would be directly over her, and if she could catch some of the white stuff she might learn what the ship's cargo was, perhaps guess at its destination. Her training as a chemist would give her a useful guide if the white trickle turned out to be chemical crystals of any kind. Intrigued, she waited, her hand outstretched and her face upraised.

'Dee, run! Get out of the way!'

She heard Nat shout. She had time to wonder why he shouted, time to feel resentment boil up inside her that he should roar at her in such an arbitrary manner, obviously expecting her to obey his order without question. Time to feel a sudden upsurge of fear pierce her sharply, rooting her to the spot as if the archer had loosed his arrow and found his mark. Then a cloud of blinding white broke directly above her. The first loose grains tickled her nose, but before she could draw breath to sneeze, hard arms grabbed her, swept her off her feet, and carried her at a headlong run safely away from the spot that, seconds later, disappeared under the entire sackful of white in a heavy, bone-shattering, choking cloud.

'Didn't you hear me shout? Why didn't you run?'

Nat swung her, none too gently, back on to her feet, and glared down at her. 'Thank goodness it was flour, and not something corrosive!' He tugged a clean folded handkerchief from his pocket and rubbed it across her face with hasty fingers. Her cheeks and forehead were white with the dusting of powder. His own face was just as white under its tan, but not from flour grains, and his eyes burned into hers with shocked fury. 'You're absolutely covered in the stuff,' he growled angrily, and ruffled quick fingers through her hair, shaking the shining gold strands free from their snowy covering. 'You might have had your neck broken, been choked. . . .'

'Make up your mind!' she flared back angrily, wriggling under his ministrations, resenting his criticism. 'I'm still alive, aren't I?' She was trembling from head to foot with the narrowness of her escape, but she was determined not to let him see it.

'You're alive, and no thanks to you,' he cut in grimly. 'What are you doing on the quay, anyway?' he demanded brusquely. 'I left you in the car.' Without waiting for her to answer he went on, 'Didn't you see the trickle of powder falling from the net?'

'Of course I did.' Surely even Nat didn't imagine she was that unobservant, she thought impatiently. 'I wanted to catch some of it, to find out what it was.'

'Give me strength!' he exploded, so fiercely that it made her jump. 'Are you so scatterbrained that you hadn't the sense to realise a leak means a damaged container?' he demanded. 'If the container's damaged in one place,' he controlled his patience with an obvious effort, 'it's likely to give way altogether without any warning, and deposit the contents on top of you if you're stupid enough to stand underneath,' he emphasised forcefully. 'Why do you think the stevedores scattered when they saw the load coming towards them?'

She had not seen the stevedores; the men had been hidden from her, as she must have been hidden from them, by the stack of unused pallets.

'How was I to know? I'm not a dock worker. The only reason I'm on the quay in the first place is because you were so long away from the car I got tired of waiting,' she flung back at him, her temper rising to match his own. 'I came looking for you.' She thrust the blame squarely back on his shoulders. It was not true, but she felt no regret until she saw the steely glint appear in his eyes.

'You couldn't have been looking for me. You had to walk right past the tug, to get near the cargo vessel,' he collapsed her excuse like a cardhouse in a gale. 'Though I suppose I shouldn't be surprised at anything,' he added sarcastically, 'with a female scatty enough to park her case in the back of someone else's truck and then accuse the driver of being a thief because he drove off with it.'

So he *had* heard her call after him at the station. He *had* noticed her case in the back of his truck, noticed her run towards him, and knew what she was running for. And still he had driven away without stopping. A wave of sheer fury rendered Dee momentarily speechless. It drained the last vestige of colour from her face, and turned her eyes almost as black as his own.

'You knew!' she accused him hotly. 'You knew all the time, and you deliberately. . . .' She choked into silence. How like a man! she told herself wrathfully. Arrogant, high-handed, doing just what he pleased with other people and other people's property, and not expecting even a whisper of protest in return. He was as bad as the creature who had walked in and taken over the job that should have rightfully belonged to her, she thought furiously. The sheer male chauvinism of it bit like acid at her pride. She trembled now from outrage as much as from fright. Men were all alike, she decided bitterly, they took it for granted that they had every right....

'I did it to teach you a lesson,' he told her coolly. 'In future, you'll remember not to park your belongings without permission in other people's vehicles.'

'I don't need anything to remind me....' she began angrily.

'But you obviously do,' he contradicted her softly, 'which is why....' His look should have warned her. So should the increased pressure of his hold upon her, but she was too incensed to notice either, until,

'This will remind you not to get near a ship when it's being unloaded,' he told her. And right in front of the group of grinning stevedores, he kissed her.

His face loomed close above her own. She raised her head, startled, tried to back away, to protest, and found she could do neither. His gold ear-ring winked derisively at her, then disappeared from her view as his lips covered hers with a firm, hard pressure, punishing her for leaving the car while his back was turned, punishing her for walking on the quay....

She tried to push against him, to thrust him away, but her arms were pinioned to her sides, preventing her. His kiss went on and on until her heart throbbed with a wild force that was almost a pain. It destroyed her ability and then her desire to resist, and set the tiny pulse spots in her throat and her delicately blue temples throbbing in sympathy, as his lips left her mouth at last and pressed on the spots to quieten them, and only succeeded in making them beat more wildly than before. And then, bereft, her lips turned impulsively to seek his again, bewailing their loss to the pulse spots, demanding that they be given precedence, with a movement of their own over which she seemed to have no control, any more than she could control the overwhelming flood of emotion aroused by the touch of his arms, the pressure of his lips, the sheer male magnetism of him that without warning washed over her, terrified her, took possession of her, so that when at last he released her and stood looking down on to her breathless, wide-eyed stare, she knew with a certainty that was almost akin to despair that life for her could never be the same again. He glanced away from her to consult his watch, looked back at her, and somewhere deep in his black eyes the familiar laughter lurked once more.

'We'll have to hurry, or we'll be too late to get your aunt's box of chocolates,' he said.

CHAPTER THREE

'GET into the front seat, next to me,' Nat ordered her peremptorily. His tone said he did not trust her by herself in the back seat. Dee noticed there was a leather camera case set on it now, that had not been there before. That must have been the reason for his visit to his cabin, to collect it.

She bridled, resenting his manner, resenting being treated like a naughty child, and being blamed for something, she told herself firmly, which was not her fault in the first place. She glanced up at him, prompted to defy him in spite of the need for haste if only to assert her independence and to let him see that she was not ready to obey his orders as meekly as he obviously expected her to. She longed to slide past him, to stalk away and prick the bubble of his arrogance, but. . . .

She bit her lip and looked across at the stevedores, burningly conscious of their interested stares as they waited for another net-load of flour bags to descend and provide them with occupation. And if she did walk away, she would not be able to get the chocolates her aunt wanted. Quite apart from the fact that she could not walk to the nearest shop in time, she had no money with her; she had left her handbag in the car. Perhaps—she eyed the distance between herself and her property calculatingly—perhaps if she was quick enough she could manage to bend down and snatch her bag, and slip away. She hesitated, but Nat took a sideways step that put him behind her, as if he sensed her intention, and foiled it before she could even try. She shrugged, defeated, and ducked under his arm, and through the door which he held open for her. Capitulation rasped her pride, and exasperation exploded into speech as Nat ducked inside the car after her and slid the seat belt securely round her, leaning right across her to clip it into its locking position on the console.

'You don't have to tie me in, I'm a passenger, not a prisoner,' she snapped. She felt trapped, stifled by his closeness as he leaned across her. Her heart hammered, and her breath came in short, panting gasps. She longed to push him away, to catch him to her. She could not make up her mind which she longed to do. Her fingers urged to run through his strong, midnight hair, to turn his face once again to her own, so that their lips could meet. A million years passed before the seat belt lock mechanism clicked, and with a lithe, easy unfolding of his long body he ducked out from the passenger compartment, straightened up, and said,

'You're also vulnerable, if I have to make an unscheduled stop. So leave the seat belt in place,' he warned, his tone hardening perceptibly as her fingers hovered mutinously over the vividly coloured release button. 'If I have to brake suddenly I don't want your pretty head shattering my windscreen.' So he acknowledged it was pretty! The thought had hardly crossed her mind when he spoiled the effect by adding, 'Windscreens are expensive to replace.' He made it plain that it was his windscreen, and not her head, that was his primary concern. 'And since you've made us late by playing catch-as-catch-can with loads of flour, I'll have to put on speed if we're to get to the shops before they close.'

'*I've* made us late?' She snatched her fingers away from the release button and curled them together convulsively, angrily, in her lap. How typical! she thought scathingly. How typical of him to blame herself, when by his own act in visiting the tug, it was Nat who had made them late. It would have been just as easy to get the chocolates first, and visit the tug for his camera on the way back.

'So hold tight,' he warned, ignoring her indignant outburst, dismissing her, she realised furiously, to put his whole attention on reversing neatly from off the narrow quayside, back up the hard, and on to the road.

In spite of her anger, she could not help feeling a reluctant admiration at his easy handling of the powerful car. She did not have to hold tight, and he did not have to make any emergency stops. He drove fast, but with a consummate skill and total concentration that foresaw the learner driver's sudden unsignalled turn to the right in front of their bonnet; judged to a nicety the canine flashpoint that sent a huge black alsatian dog snarling across the road towards an equally tall boxer growling challenges from the opposite pavement, the former dragging its hapless owner along with it at the other end of its lead, to the hazard of life and limb.

'Untrained dog owners. . . .' Nat commented critically, apportioning blame where it belonged, but before Dee had time to let out a relieved breath at the narrow escape, let alone reply, he pulled the car to a smooth halt beside the town's best confectionery shop, with several minutes to spare before six o'clock. He undid his own seat belt and left his seat with no particular appearance of haste, but sixty seconds later he returned bearing a large, beribboned box of a popular brand of chocolates with, Dee could not resist a peep inside the bag, a bright Alpine scene decorating the front.

It was exactly what her aunt wanted. She should have been delighted that he had succeeded in obtaining it, if only for that reason. Just as she should have derived pleasure from his superb driving. Within the big car there was no sensation of speed, their progression assumed a deceptively leisurely eating of the miles back towards Cliff House, and it was only when she glanced at the speedometer that she received a shock. The reading underlined the competence of the driver, and if it had been anyone else but Nat at the wheel she would have watched, marvelled and tried to learn in the hope of emulating his prowess in her own performance when the garage eventually returned her car. As it was she merely felt an irrational surge of irritation with both the chocolates and Nat's driving, which vented itself in angry speech when he pulled up at the gate and allowed her to carry the chocolates, but calmly refused to hand her the bill for them.

'I want to know how much,' she demanded, and held out her hand imperiously for the bill. 'It's my place to pay....'

'On the contrary,' he coolly filled her outstretched fingers with her discarded gloves which she had left forgotten on the parcel shelf in the car, 'on the contrary, it's your aunt's place to pay, since she asked for the chocolates. I'll settle with her.'

But after he left nearly an hour later, she discovered he had omitted to do so. Her aunt insisted on inviting him in and plying him with tea and cake which even at that late hour in the evening he consumed with every evidence of enjoyment, until Dee began to think he would never go and leave her to start cooking the dinner in peace. To her relief he shook his head at her aunt's invitation to remain for the main meal.

'I'll give him cheese on toast, if he does,' she planned darkly, but he was adamant in his refusal, and after a second slice of home-made cake, on which he complimented her aunt on her baking—he did not repeat the compliment when he was told it was Dee who had baked it, she noticed—he took his leave.

'He can go on his own, I won't see him off,' she vowed inhospitably, but the wirehaired terrier unexpectedly obliged her to change her mind. The moment the car engine started the little dog took off with a shrill yap, evading her clutching fingers as it raced towards the car to 'see it off', a game of which it never seemed to tire, whether it was barking at birds or motor cars. It was a noisy but harmless enthusiasm when it was confined to the gulls, but before his injury her uncle had taken stern measures to curb the young dog's habit of chasing vehicles. Dee tried to carry on with the discipline, and was singularly unsuccessful, as she was now.

'Skip, come back!' Not for the first time she discovered that four short legs could easily outstrip two much longer ones, and by the time she reached the gate the little terrier was already snapping at the car's front wheels.

'You'll get yourself killed!' she scolded, and ran towards the yapping dog, grabbing ineffectually as it dodged the car wheels and her grasp with maddening ease.

'And so will you, if you're silly enough to run into the path of a car to try and rescue the little beast.'

With a speed that made her blink, Nat slammed on the brake, killed the engine, and in a single angry movement got out of the car and grabbed the terrier.

'Let that be a lesson to you!' He administered a hard spank with the flat of his hand, which changed the yaps to a yelp, and brought a torrent of protest from Dee.

'How dare you hit him?' she stormed. 'He's little more than a puppy.' If it had been anyone else but Nat, she would have acknowledged him justified. But not Nat.

'I did it because he deserved it,' he growled back angrily. 'If he isn't checked he won't live to grow up. And if you run in front of my wheels again,' he added warningly to Dee, 'I might be tempted to give you the same treatment.' His black-browed scowl told her he would not be above carrying out his threat, might even do so now if. . . . Her eyes widened, and she took a step backwards.

'Don't dare lay hands on me!' she breathed furiously.

'I won't—this time,' he said significantly. 'Now take a tight hold of him,' he bent and scooped up the terrier, and dumped the subdued dog into her arms, 'and don't let go of him until the car's out of sight.'

'He's a very forceful young man,' her aunt commented, when Dee returned to the house and related what had happened, but she did not sound in the least critical.

TUG OF WAR

'He's a big, overbearing bully,' Dee contradicted wrathfully, and gave the young terrier a reassuring cuddle before she set him free.

'Your uncle would probably have done the same thing,' her aunt replied mildly, with what Dee felt uncomfortably was more than a grain of truth. 'Skip's got out of hand since the accident, he'll simply have to lose the habit of chasing vehicles, he could cause a collision one day.'

'He just ran into one himself, with Nat's hand,' Dee interposed drily. The sound of the slap made her wince even now, to remember it.

'Perhaps it'll make him think twice in future,' Skip's owner said hopefully, and added, 'Now if you'll give me my purse I'll pay you back for the chocolates. You couldn't have chosen a nicer box,' she added happily.

'I didn't choose it, Nat did,' Dee replied shortly. 'And he wouldn't let me pay for it, he said he'd settle with you.'

'It must have slipped his memory.' Dee knew that it had not. 'You can pay him the next time you meet—I expect you'll be seeing him again soon.'

'Not if I can help it,' Dee vowed silently. And the next day she found that, once again, the choice was taken out of her hands.

'Helen won't be long before she's here to pick you up.' Dee looked at her watch after lunch the following afternoon. 'I'll take the boat and go along the creek, I can use the time to gather the shells I promised the therapist.'

'Can you manage the outboard motor?' her aunt queried, and Dee nodded.

'I should think so,' she replied confidently. 'It isn't very much different from the one on the motor mower.' Since staying at Cliff House, she had conscientiously kept the lawns neatly shaven, until she felt quite at home with the small engine.

'What about Skip?' Her aunt looked slightly uneasy.

'I'll take him along with me. I can keep an eye on him then,' Dee decided. 'He can bark as much as he likes at the outboard motor, without coming to any harm,' she smiled. 'In fact, it might be wiser to go before Helen arrives, I don't want a repeat of yesterday's performance when he hears her car.' The terrier's antics had frightened her more than she was willing to admit, and Nat's explosive reaction had frightened her more still.

'Come on, let's go.' She picked up a string bag in which reposed a large roll of cotton wool ready to receive the shells, and snapped her fingers to the willing terrier. 'Helen must be almost here.' She cast an apprehensive glance along the road before she opened the gate and loosed Skip's collar. The car was nowhere to be seen, but it might at any moment breast the rise, and then. . . .

'This way!' she called. Rather than risk another confrontation she turned on to the narrow track that wound almost vertically down the cliff face to the cove below. 'The smugglers must have been a hardy lot, to hump casks of brandy up here,' she paid respectful tribute to the toughness of the long-ago law-breakers, and felt thankful she had thought to put on tennis pumps as something that would not be spoiled by her afternoon beachcombing. They provided her with a much-needed grip on the steep, uneven track. 'Be thankful you've got four feet,' she told Skip, who found no difficulty in keeping his balance, and regarded the whole outing as an adventure. Dee loosed the string bag and let it slide on ahead of her, then used both hands as brakes on the clumps of heather and thrift growing alongside the track. 'Thank goodness there's no one below in the cove!' she thought. Safe from watching eyes, she could let her bright poppy red cotton skirt blow about her bare brown legs, unchecked in the mischievous breeze. She sat down and slid the last few feet, and ended in a rush on the shingle below.

'We'll have to come back the other way, I don't fancy climbing that after an afternoon gathering shells.' She paused for a moment to get her breath back, and pick off prickles of furze that had adhered to her sleeveless white top in the last hectic rush to the beach.

'Skip, come back! You'll get the cotton wool wet.' The terrier brought her rest to an abrupt end by gripping the string bag in his teeth and dancing away with it towards the water's edge, and Dee raced in the dog's wake. 'Here, Skip! Fetch it, boy!' She bent and tossed a pebble to distract the miscreant, and breathed a sigh of relief as her ploy succeeded. The terrier dropped the bag and ran off after her missile.

'Making off with my belongings seems to be getting a habit around here,' she told herself ruefully, and slipped off her pumps and dropped them in the bag preparatory to wading out into the warm shallows to where the skiff rode at anchor on the sun-bright water. Her spirits lifted. It was a perfect day, and she had the whole afternoon to herself. It was just what she needed, she decided, to calm her down and make her see things in perspective. Make her see Nat in perspective? Her mind shied away from the thought of him.

'I'm not going to let him spoil today,' she told herself firmly. 'I've let the man get under my skin.' No man had ever succeeded in doing that before, and it hurt her pride that Nat had accomplished it with such seeming ease. Honesty reminded her that he had managed to penetrate much deeper. His image laughed up at her now from the dappled shallows, loomed over her from the frowning cliffs. It was no use shutting her eyes, she had tried that before, and she could not shut him out. She thrust honesty ruthlessly away from her, and excused herself out loud.

'It's because I'm upset, that's all. It's all the upheaval, what with Uncle's accident, and the bother about my job. I'll settle down and forget him as soon as I take over the other lab in the autumn,' she assured herself staunchly, and shrugged away the unease which reminded her painfully that, although leaving Penzyn would mean leaving

Nat behind, she could not dispense with her memory so easily. His face would still have the power to haunt her....

'Come here, Skip, I'll give you a lift into the boat. I don't want you shaking water all over me.' She tucked the terrier under her arm, and transferred him safely into the skiff, then climbed in after him, glad of action to divert her thoughts.

'Goodness, this is stiff!' The pull start on the outboard was a lot harder than the one on the mowing machine, she discovered, and she regarded the still silent engine with dismay. It had looked so easy, when she watched her uncle bring the engine into life at the first pull on the cord. 'I won't have my afternoon spoiled,' she muttered stubbornly, and took hold of the start cord with both hands. 'Stand clear,' she warned the terrier humorously, and put all her strength into one mighty heave.

The engine started with a bang. The loud explosion startled Dee into dropping the cord, and set the terrier yapping, and the combination of fright and din stepped her hastily backwards. She forgot that she was afloat. The boat reminded her by rocking wildly at her incautious movement, which was all that was needed to upset her balance completely. She flailed her arms in a desperate attempt to remain on her feet, and lost the unequal battle in an undignified collapse into the bottom of the skiff. The terrier decided it was the signal for a romp, and with shrill yaps it jumped on top of her, and in the ensuing mêlée the cotton wool somehow managed to escape the confinement of the string bag, and by the time Dee regained her seat, slowed the engine to a more reasonable beat, and quietened the terrier, the hapless white roll was already floating out of reach, rapidly absorbing water until, weighted down, it sank beyond recall.

'Now look what you've done!' Dee raised her voice above the engine and shouted at the chastened Skip.

'You naughty dog!' Without the cotton wool to wrap them in, there was a risk that any shells she gathered might become chipped, and she was anxious that her gift to the therapist should be in perfect condition. 'It's high time you were taken in hand,' she scolded, and felt thankful that Nat was nowhere within earshot. Not for the world would she have him know that she shared his feelings anent the terrier.

She did not know what made her look upwards. Perhaps it was that sixth sense that civilisation has never been quite able to erase, that instinctive inner awareness of when something, or somebody, is watching. Unerringly, Dee's eyes flew straight to the silent watcher on the cliff top. He stood at the start of the smugglers' track, looking down on her. How long he had been there she had no means of knowing. Her startled eyes travelled upwards across black slacks, black rollneck sweater, black hair, and, even at this distance, the bright glint of the sun striking the gold ear-ring in his right ear.

She caught her breath, and a tingle of conflicting emotions shivered through her, one of which was fear. She did not stop to analyse the rest, or to question the reason that brought Nat to the cliff top. With an abrupt movement that set the boat rocking again, so that she had to stoop quickly and grab the side to prevent another spill, she turned her back on him and set the skiff in motion. He must have heard her shout at the terrier, and her cheeks burned at the satisfaction he would be feeling now because of it.

'Let him gloat,' she muttered crossly, and brought the boat about, and pointed it out to the end of the headland. Her route lay around the point to the mouth of the creek hidden in the steeply wooded banks that dipped their feet in the water's edge on the other side of the promontory. The move kept her back turned towards the cliffs, and Nat, if he was still there. With a great effort of will she resisted the urge to turn her head and look behind her to find out. She could feel his eyes burn into her back, recording her every movement.

'I wish I was in the fishing smack.' She wriggled her shoulders, unable to shake off the unease of feeling herself under observation. In the smack she would at least have had the wheelhouse to shelter in, and the illusion of privacy. Out on the water in the skiff she felt as conspicuous as a fly on a wall, and just about as vulnerable. Without conscious reasoning, she reached out and increased the pace of the engine, sending the boat surging forward at unnecessary speed round the headland towards the dark brooding woods on the far shore—running for the shelter of the trees, as a creature of the wild runs for cover to escape the hunter.

'I'm not afraid of Nat,' she assured herself. But if she was not afraid, why did she run? Despite her self-derision, she could not bring herself to cut the speed of the engine, and she heaved a sigh of pure relief as the boat turned into the mouth of the creek and the trees closed in behind her, shutting her off from sight of the watcher on the shore. She eased the engine then and let the boat glide slowly along the waterway while she sat back and relaxed in her seat, to discover she was trembling.

'I *have* let him get under my skin.' A frown creased her face, like the shadows cast by the overhanging trees. They blotted out the sun, but it was not entirely their cool shade that made her feel so suddenly cold.

'Oh, forget Nat,' she scolded herself, irritable with the release from tension. 'You're allowing him to play on your nerves.' She ran the boat out of the shelter of the woods to where the trees receded and the creek widened on to a small beach. 'Now you can play as much as you like,' she told the eager terrier, and raised her face to the grateful warmth of the sun again. The creek forked here, giving two entrances to the sea, so that on the map they looked like two crooked legs, and where the currents converged on the inside curve of the small bay, the beach shone whitely, built up over who knew how many centuries by the shells of the minute sea creatures that came to breed in the sheltered waters. Time had ground their delicate, discarded homes into a fine powder which gleamed like mother-of-pearl in the sunshine. A pair of swans sailed majestically near by, leading a flotilla of dowdy cygnets, completing the idyllic—and, she saw, thankfully—deserted scene.

'Thank goodness I've got it to myself.' She was unrepentantly selfish. She did not want company, any company, this afternoon. She ran the boat on to the beach and secured it with a line to a nearby exposed tree root. A gleam of pale blue caught her attention among the trees, and she recognised the local grocer's van. She knew it came along the creek road twice a week to serve the two small hamlets there. The driver had probably stopped to look at the swans. The patch of blue moved away even as she watched, and she returned to the boat, satisfied that she was alone.

'You can do just what you like, short of chewing my tennis pumps,' she told Skip magnanimously. 'I want those to put the shells in, I've got nothing else now the cotton wool's gone.' The beach made for soft walking, and she went happily barefoot. For a while the terrier followed her until he lost interest in shells, and wandered off in search of more interesting things. Dee lost count of time. The silence washed round her like a benediction, calming her nerves, soothing her irritation away. The swans remained close by, probing the shallows, teaching their brood to feed, their busy activity adding to rather than detracting from the tranquillity of the spot.

Dee moved slowly, curling her toes in the warm shell dust, stooping to pick a shell here, a shell there, holding them up to watch the light play on their varied colours, marvelling at their beauty and form. Soon she had more than her hand could comfortably hold, and rather than risk chipping them she transferred them to her skirt, and held it up in front of her as an impromptu scoop. The tide had been out for some time, and the shells were clean and dry.

'There's no one here to see my petticoats.' She blessed the fact that there were no onlookers, although the white cotton broderie anglaise threaded through with scarlet ribbon to match the skirt on top could only draw admiration if there were. The shells made a delicate pattern against their poppy red background, the sun was hot, and she felt suddenly, gloriously free. With a gay little laugh she raised her face to the bright rays, held her skirt up high, and twirled in a swift, abandoned dance across the beach, leaving circlets in the pale shell sand, and stirring the bright ribbons of her underskirt into fluttering life.

A mechanical click, a cacophony of yapping, and an enraged hiss shattered the silence all at the same time. Dee stopped dead, in mid-twirl. Her arms dropped, her skirt released its burden, and the shells trickled back to the beach from whence they came. Her startled eyes flew to the source of the click. Nat removed the camera from his eye, spun the film ready for the next shot, and strolled casually towards her.

'All the best photographs are the unrehearsed ones,' he grinned.

'How dare you take my picture?' She recovered from the shock, and stormed into angry speech. Her cheeks took on the colour of her skirt, and she forgot the small pile of shells lying forlornly at her feet. 'You've no right ... I didn't give you permission ... you're not to publish it.' She stammered to a confused halt, torn between fury at his action, and embarrassment at what the camera must have recorded.

'Acres of bare leg, and yards of petticoat,' her mind told her with pitiless honesty. Her eyes widened with dismay at the thought, and she burst out furiously, 'I won't have my picture used as a calendar pin-up!' She did not know if

Nat took pictures for calendars, but it was a risk she was not prepared to take. 'I won't, do you hear?' She longed to strike the grin from his face, shake the cool assumption that he could do what he liked without bothering to ask permission first. 'I'll . . . I'll. . . . Skip, stop it! Come back!' Her cry turned to an agonised shout as the yaps grew more intense, and the angry hiss was joined by an even angrier flapping, and confused splashing sounds. The latter were caused by the frightened cygnets retreating across the shallows in complete disarray in front of the gleefully yapping terrier, which was too intent on enjoying the successful rout of yet another kind of bird to notice the angry cob rise tall on its webbed feet, wings flapping and neck outstretched, intent on wreaking vengeance on the rash intruder.

'He'll be hurt . . . drowned. . . .' She forgot the shells, the photograph, even Nat.

'Dee. . . .' He reached out, grasping at her, but she dodged his outstretched arm, did not wait to hear what it was he wanted to say, and sped with the fleetness of a gazelle across the beach to the water's edge. Without a pause she ran straight into the shallows, heedless of where the bright drops flew. They spattered her skirt, her hair, her face. . . .

'Skip, come back!' She was almost within reach of the dog. The outraged swan was almost within reach of her when Nat grabbed her. He picked her up and swung her high in his arms as the cob attacked. Tiny black eyes glittered vengefully, and a hard orange beak struck at the spot where her bare legs had stood just a moment before. Without a pause, Nat spun round and regained the beach in two long strides.

'Put me down! Let me go! Skip will get hurt.' She hammered at his chest with balled fists, her bare feet kicking ineffectually at the air as she struggled to be free. 'The swan will attack him!' Her voice choked on a sob, and she twisted frantically in his arms, her terrified eyes seeking the terrier, who seemed to have disappeared in a welter of wings and splashes and noise.

'Let him take his punishment for once. I'll intervene if it's necessary.' Nat kept a determined hold on her, checking her struggles with ease. 'It's high time that pup was taught a lesson,' he added feelingly.

'You beast! You'll enjoy seeing him hurt....' She was crying with a vengeance now. 'Skip, Skip,' she sobbed wildly, her tears blinding her to the sudden hardening of Nat's face, even to the wet white ball that was the terrier, as soaked as the cotton wool that Dee had lost earlier, as he came tumbling out of the water, his tail between his legs, racing for sanctuary just ahead of the punishing beak that exacted one more pained yelp before the cob, with the air of one having successfully dealt with an impertinent incomer, calmly folded its wings and floated out into deep water, where its small family was already peacefully gathered, safe from assault from the shore.

'Is he hurt?' Dee whispered fearfully, not daring to look at the dog as Nat tipped her back on to her feet.

'Does he look as if he is?' he asked impatiently, with a stern glance at the terrier, now busily shaking himself free from water, and with its ears and tail once more in their accustomed perky vertical position. 'It's to be hoped he's learned his lesson this time,' he added callously.

'You're a....'

'A beast. So you told me.' There was sudden steel in his voice, and it brought her face up in a startled stare, that faltered before the unexpected glint in his black eyes, that could have been anger, or.... Her gold tipped lashes dropped, and a hot tide of colour, that had nothing to do with her earlier indignant glow, spread in a rich rose across her throat and cheeks.

'I—I....' She stammered, and turned, and found herself still held within the circle of his arms. Her colour deepened, and she raised her face to his again, this time in protest. 'Let me....' She did not have time to finish. She tried to raise her arms, and found them trapped at her sides by Nat's. She tried to step backwards, but his hands linked behind her back in an unbreakable chain, and with the same deceptive lack of haste that seemed to characterise all his movements, but which nevertheless gave her no time to twist her face away, he lowered his head.

'Beauty and the beast,' he murmured mockingly.

The mere touch of one pair of lips on another should not have the power to arouse such an electrifying response; Dee's scientific training denied that such a thing was possible. It was all a simple matter of chemistry. It had to be. . . . But the eager, maturing woman in her, so long dormant, subservient to the exacting demands of her job, acknowledged joyfully that this was no mere chemistry. Her heart, her pulses, the very blood in her veins sang with a wild song she had never heard before. It was worse, far worse, than when Nat had kissed her on the harbour wall. Then, anger and shock had sheltered her. But now the siren singing chained her, mesmerised her, and she could not struggle free. This time his lips were firm, pressing against her own, but not hard, not driven by anger and shock as they had been the day before, whatever the glint in his eyes might mean now. Instead, they caressed the smile-crease at the corner of her mouth; explored the dimple in the middle of her cheek; travelled lightly across her eyes, her hair, and returned again to her lips, tasting their sweetness as a connoisseur sips fine wine, savouring its fullness, its bouquet. They drew a whisper from her throbbing throat.

'Nat . . . Nat. . . .' Miraculously, her arms were free. They rose to clasp his head and draw it tighter down to her own.

'Your lips are salty.' He did not seem to mind the salt.

'Do you want a lift back to Penzyn or not, Mr Archer? I'm in a fair hurry, so. . . .'

The driver of the blue van must have been in a frantic hurry, Dee decided, or else he had no soul. His shout from the roadway above them pricked the bubble of the golden afternoon. It brought her back to rude realities, like bare feet, a wet dog, and time. Time to go back home.

'No, thanks, I've got a lift.' Nat sent the man packing, but the moment was lost, destroyed for ever.

'My shells!' Dee had forgotten her shells. Now she remembered the reason why she had come.

'I'll help you to pick them up.' He helped her, in silence, neither of them looking at the other. Did he regret kissing her? she wondered miserably, and watched his sensitive fingers handling the delicate, fan-shaped shells are carefully as she handled them herself, as aware of the need not to chip them, even though she had not spoken of it.

'I haven't got anywhere to put them. I lost the roll of cotton wool.'

'I know—I saw.'

'Your camera case? I could use your camera case.' She knew, even as she said it, that it was a stupid thing to ask. She opened her mouth to retract.

'No,' he refused her instantly. 'If grit gets into the mechanism, it could do untold damage. Use your tennis pumps instead. We can beach the boat by the promenade on the way back, and get another roll of cotton wool from the chemist there.'

Dee put the shells into her tennis pumps, as she intended to do in the first place, but childishly resentful that Nat had not allowed her to use his camera case, knowing that it would be madness to do so, to risk what even her untutored eyes told her was a highly efficient, and hideously expensive, piece of equipment, the tool of a professional, far beyond the realms of an amateur.

He lifted Skip into the boat, helped Dee to get in, and when she was seated undid the painter from the tree root. He was in the boat and seated himself, before she realised he had put her into the passenger seat and himself at the tiller. His calm assumption of the role of owner in her uncle's boat galled her into speech.

TUG OF WAR

'I'll steer.'

She started to rise to her feet to take over the tiller, but the boat rocked violently with her sudden, angry movement. It spilled Skip against her legs, and she dropped down on to the seat again abruptly, and staccato stutter of the engine drowned her words. Nat gave the start cord a sharp pull and immediately reached for the tiller handle. He did not look back at the engine, she noticed, as if it did not occur to him that it would do anything other than obey his wish to start. How like Nat, to assume it would obey him! she thought wrathfully, chagrined by the very fact that it did, and instantly. She had had to pull the cord several times, and use both hands. Nat merely flicked it once, with an easy wrist, and let it go. She humped crossly on to the hard wooden board seat, conscious for the first time of her wet feet and legs, and liberally splashed skirt.

Nat nosed the boat out into the centre of the creek, and surprisingly the swans cruised alongside them, less than a yard away, seeming not to connect the boat with the earlier, aggressive behaviour of the terrier.

'Sit still,' Dee warned Skip anxiously, as he wriggled under the seats to the middle of the boat, out of her own reach, but still near enough for Nat to grab him, she saw thankfully.

'Change over, I'll steer.' She asserted her right to manage the boat, and Nat glanced across at her without speaking. His silence, his cool indifference to her demand, sparked the anger that lurked just underneath the surface, and she flared, 'It's not your boat. You're begging the lift this time, not me. I didn't drive your car....' It was childish, unreasonable, and she could not help it. 'If you don't change over, I'll....' His continuing silence drove her temper to breaking point, and her eyes lit on his camera, carefully placed in the bottom of the boat near to her hand. 'I'll drop this overboard,' she threatened impulsively. With quick fingers she snatched the camera strap and held the instrument high, over the side of the boat. Over deep water, where, if she dropped it, he would have the utmost difficulty in recovering it, and it would be irretrievably soaked even if he did.

He looked across at her, out of quickly narrowed eyes, and she knew she had gone too far. His look kindled, his face tightened, and for a brief moment he held her eyes with his own and she went cold all over. Then he reached over unhurriedly and picked up the terrier by his middle.

'If you drop my camera,' he said in an even voice, 'I'll drop him.' And he held the dog over the side of the boat, over equally deep water, and almost within reach of the swans. As if to emphasise his threat the cob swung round to face them, the sight of the terrier bringing the long white neck forward in a threatening gesture. 'I'll drop the dog,' Nat warned coolly, and added as an afterthought, 'and for two pins, I'll drop you in after him.'

CHAPTER FOUR

STALEMATE!

The swan stretched out a long neck. The dog whined, and Nat's jaw set in a square, uncompromising line. The cob settled the matter. It gave vent to a hiss like a snake, and headed straight for the boat and the dog with a powerful stroke of its great webbed feet. Dee's nerve broke.

'Put Skip back!' she cried hastily. 'I won't drop your camera.'

She gave a frightened gulp and drew the instrument inboard, laying it to rest on the bottom of the boat where it had been before. She would have liked to drop it on the boat boards, hard, she thought furiously. Not hard enough to do it permanent damage, she had too great a respect for fine instruments to do that, but hard enough to crack the lens so that the next time Nat opened the case it would let in sufficient light to spoil that part of the film that bore her image. She hesitated for a vital second, her eyes on his face, and he returned her look with one of steel. It told her quite clearly that he was aware of the thoughts that were crossing her mind. It also invited her to go ahead, if she dared, and risk the retribution that would surely follow.

She did not dare. She let out a slow breath and lowered the camera gently on to the boat boards, hating the derision in his eyes. He had anticipated her reaction, perhaps even despised her for it, for being weak.

'I don't care,' she told herself passionately. 'I don't care for him, so what he thinks of me doesn't matter. Now give me Skip,' she added out loud, keeping Nat to his side of the bargain.

'You can have him, and welcome.' He deliberately dropped the still wet terrier squarely into her lap, effectively soaking bits of her skirt that were not already splashed.

'Beast!' she flashed, too angry to be cautious. Hastily she removed the dog to the bottom of the boat, but it was too late to save her skirt. 'He can sit on your camera instead,' she spat furiously, but Nat had already stretched out a long arm and drawn his property out of reach, and setting the boat in motion he steered it towards the narrow exit from the creek. As soon as the dog disappeared from sight the swan lost interest, and rejoined its family, and Dee hunched back on the hard board seat and tried not to shiver as the cool shade of the trees struck chill through her wet skirt. It cooled her skin, but not her temper, and she simmered in resentful silence as Nat skilfully manoeuvred the skiff out of the narrow creek and back into the bay, and pointed it towards the distant shoreline. Dee kept her head averted from him, stubbornly refusing to look at him, but finding it almost impossible not to. Try as she might she could not ignore his presence opposite to her, every nerve end of her was throbbingly conscious of him, reacting to him, as a pin reacts to a powerful magnet, unable to help itself.

'I'll get a crick in my neck if I don't look the other way soon,' she decided desperately, then voluntarily turned her head even further still, startled into realisation that the shoreline should have been a good deal closer by now than it was. Far from heading towards it, Nat was deliberately keeping the boat parallel with the cliffs, and a good way out. He seemed to be heading for the point of the peninsula.

'We're going the wrong way.' Dee turned and looked at him then, and her eyes snapped. She should have insisted on taking over the tiller herself, as was her right, she told herself stormily. She should have *made* him give it up to her.

'How?' reality asked her jeeringly, bidding her contrast Nat's six foot plus of hard muscle with her own diminutive stature.

'I should have done something, found some way.' She was in no mood to listen to reason, let alone reality.

'I told you we'd call at the chemist on the promenade on the way back, and get another roll of cotton wool for your shells,' he answered her coolly.

He had told her, he had not asked her. And now he was doing as he said he intended to, and carrying her along with him whether she wanted to go or not.

'I want to go ashore here, from where I started out. I don't want to go right round to the promenade,' she stated flatly.

'You'll find it a long swim ashore from here.' His eyes glinted, acknowledging the confrontation, unmoved by it, treating it with the cool disdain of a St Bernard turning to look at a yapping Pekinese. 'It's nearly a mile,' he calculated the distance with narrowed eyes. Measuring how far? Or laughing at her? Inviting her to swim ashore if she wanted to, but telling her that was the only way she would reach land until he chose to run the boat in. Telling her he had no intention of deviating from his chosen course, and she could either go along with him, or. . . .

'You . . . you. . . .!' There was nothing in her entire vocabulary that fitted him, she decided wrathfully, and before she had the opportunity to think of anything even remotely applicable, he went on reflectively, as if she had not spoken,

'It'll be rough walking, in bare feet across the cliff. Even if you miss out the smugglers' track there's still a lot of heather and scrub on the easy route to the top. Unless you intend to carry your pumps with you?' he asked her interestedly. 'Though you risk losing your shells if you do.'

She risked losing the shells anyway. Her hands shook so much as she picked up her pumps that she risked spilling their precious contents as she followed Nat angrily up the long sloping beach towards the promenade. She had not got any money with her, and she did not intend him to pay for the cotton wool as well as for the chocolates. For the moment he would have to, but if she went with him she would at least know how much it was, so that she could reimburse him afterwards. She was quite determined to pay him back. To be in Nat's debt even for a short time galled unbearably.

He took not the slightest notice of her angry protest at being carried to the opposite side of the town, and a wave of fury flooded over her at the memory of the way in which he calmly steered towards the point he wanted to reach as if she had not even spoken. She felt she would gladly capsize the boat, rather than let him carry her an inch beyond where she wanted to go. She longed to fling her pumps, her shells—yes, even the dog, anything to remove the calmly commanding look from Nat's face that accepted her acquiescence as a matter of course, not questioning that his own decision could be anything but the right one. Not questioning that she would fall in with whatever he decided to do. She wanted to scream, shout, grasp the side of the boat and rock it with all her strength until it rolled right over, rather than allow Nat to have his own way. Instead, helpless frustration kept her rigidly still, suppressing the flood of furious words that longed to run tumbling from her lips, and they rounded the point and joined the flotilla of hired holiday boats from the beach, and she remained angrily silent, and allowed the scalding resentment to simmer inside her and do dreadful things to her emotions, because she would not allow herself to use the only safety valve left to her, because she knew with horrid certainty that it would not have the slightest effect if she did.

'Let's roll the shells in the cotton wool, then you can

wear your pumps to go back home.' Nat stripped the blue wrapping paper from the newly acquired roll, crumpled it into a ball between his fingers, and dropped it neatly into a nearby waste paper basket.

'Never mind the shells, I'll do them on the way back,' Dee sharply rejected his suggestion before she had even time to consider it.

'It's better to do it here than trying to do it on the boat. We can spread the roll out on top of the wall and place the shells in whatever pattern you want to display them. It'll save having to do them twice.'

It was so eminently reasonable, so right. It was the thing that, left to herself, she would have done as a matter of course. But because Nat suggested it, she sought for an excuse—any excuse would do—not to comply. Deliberately she dropped her tennis pumps on to a nearby wooden bench, on the side away from Nat, and tried to think of some other way of carrying the shells. She would have to wear the pumps to go up the cliff; it would be impossible, as Nat said, to walk through the heather, or even up the smugglers' track, without them. She frowned, her mind darting here and there, her eyes staring unseeing at the busy activity on the beach.

'Leave them alone!' Nat's stern warning broke across her thoughts, and her eyes swivelled back to her tennis pumps just in time to see Skip reach up and grasp at the dangling laces with his teeth.

'Don't!' In a panic she grabbed at the dog, the pumps, but the terrier had already desisted. Perversely, he obeyed Nat without question. Perversely, Dee wished Skip had grabbed her pumps and made off with them, defying him. Instead, the terrier sat down meekly, with its head on one side, obedient, but not at all abashed.

'Oh, have the shells if you want them. They'll be easier to carry in the roll.' She capitulated grudgingly, and shook the shells on to the top of the wall, trying not to see Nat's well cut lips tilt upwards at her ungracious surrender. He unrolled the cotton wool on the flat top of the stonework and asked casually,

'How would you like them placed?'

'Don't tell me you haven't got any ideas of your own?' she flashed back sarcastically, and his teeth gleamed whitely in his tanned face.

'I thought of placing them this way....' She did not intend him to do the placing, she intended to do it for herself, if only to prevent Nat from taking charge of that as well, but to her chagrin he took her comment as an invitation and reached for the shells. She stood beside him, fuming in silence, refusing to watch, then curiosity overcame her, and she looked down to see what he was doing.

'I want them to look nice, to be presentable,' she began critically, then stopped. The shells looked nice. They looked more than presentable. Most men would have jumbled them higgledy-piggledy on to the cotton wool, their only criterion being the safe transportation. Nat made pictures with them. With a sensitive artistry that dissipated her anger, roused her to reluctant admiration, and drew from her an unwilling gasp, 'That's beautiful!' he made pictures with her shells on the soft white background. Before her wondering eyes a delicate Japanese fan appeared; a crinoline lady and a parasol; a tree, a flower.

'We've run out of cotton wool,' he mourned.

'And shells.' Dee mourned too. Their eyes met, for the first time in accord.

'Let's have an ice cream.' He rolled the cotton wool back into its original shape, bulkier now because of the shells, and bought two ice creams from the beach hut.

'You don't deserve it, but I can't leave you out.' Nat shared a corner of his wafer with the terrier, unable to resist its pleading whine.

'You'll get fat.' Dee gave in, too, and they both laughed at the little dog's enjoyment.

'We probably look like a married couple.' She did not

know why the thought should cross her mind. It just did. They strolled together across the beach towards the boat, with the dog in tow, just like any of the dozens of holiday-makers crowding the stretch of golden sand. They paused to watch a Punch and Judy show, children again for the moment, until Dee happened to look up and caught Nat watching her, and there was nothing childlike in his eyes or his expression as he studied the play of laughter and shadow across her mobile face while the puppets locked in their endless battle that never changed, and neither seemed to win.

'They behave just like Nat and me. We never meet but we quarrel. Only Nat always wins. . . .'

The laughter fled from her eyes, and the shadows stayed, and the brief carefree sojourn into childhood was over. In silence, she shook white shell sand from out of her tennis pumps.

'I'll sit down and put these on before we go back to the boat,' she said out loud.

'Don't sit down here, the sand's wet.' As usual Nat found a perfectly logical reason for preventing her from doing what she wanted to, she thought resentfully. And as usual, he was right. Pools trapped by the breakwater promised her an inhospitable seat if she risked defying him. 'I'll hold you, while you stand on one leg.'

She would rather have risked the wet sand. Rivers of water could not hope to quench the burning flame that coursed through her at his touch. It turned her veins to liquid fire, set her nerve ends tingling to the tips of her sand-browned toes, and made her head reel so that she swayed against him as she tried to balance on one leg so that he need not hold her, need not touch her. Her heart thumped with a slow drumbeat of warning that seemed to find an echo in the wild scream of the gulls that cruised overhead.

'You've got no sense of balance,' he chided, and there was amusement in his voice as he held her upright, with his hands around her waist while she shook sand from tennis pumps she could no longer see because of the sudden, scalding tears that blocked her vision. She tugged her footwear on to her feet, regardless of the fact that the latter were still covered with sand, and she risked a blister by walking in them as they were. Blisters were not important. Life was not important against the illogical longing that possessed her to turn into his arms, clasp her hands round his neck, and feel his lips once more upon her own. She fumbled blindly with the laces, while her heart cried out within her,

'Nat, Nat, I love you.'

And her mind made her voice say prosaically,

'That'll do for now. I'll manage until we get home.'

She wiped her eyes quickly as Nat turned to call to the dog, and nearly managed to tuck her handkerchief out of sight back into her pocket before he turned towards her again, but he saw, and she said hurriedly, to avert a question,

'A bit of sand got in my eye, I think. It's gone now,' she added, equally hurriedly. She dared not let him ask to see, perhaps take her face in his hands to have a closer look. She dared not let him touch her again, or else she would not be able to hide the tears that flowed from her bewildered heart and threatened to overwhelm her.

'Come on, Skip, I'll race you to the boat.' Panic gripped her and she took to her heels, running for the boat, running blindly away from Nat. Afraid of him, but even more afraid of herself, of her own reactions to the man whom a few days ago she had not even met. The terrier joined in the race with noisy enjoyment, and they reached the boat together, and Dee turned to find Nat hard on her heels. She raised shining eyes to his, but she was not afraid now that he would guess the reason. He would think the shine came from the excitement of the race.

'Jump in.' He bent to lift the dog, and Dee scrambled

aboard herself, frantic to get in the boat before he could give her a helping hand too. Without thinking she sat down on the passenger seat, leaving the tiller to Nat. He slid off his own sandals, rolled up his trouser legs, and waded out into the shallows, pushing the boat in front of him, the muscles standing up like cords under the mahogany skin of his arms until the skiff floated free, and he vaulted lightly aboard and pulled the engine into life, giving her a long, hard look as he took the tiller and steered a course for the tip of the peninsula again, perhaps wondering at her sudden lack of desire to claim the disputed tiller. He could not know of the tears that blocked her throat, denying her speech, while her heart cried out so loudly with anguish that she wondered dully why he did not hear.

'This is madness,' she told herself, aghast. After she left Penzyn to take up her new job in the autumn, she would never see Nat again. Come to that, he might leave before she did, when whatever brought him and his tug into harbour had been repaired or renewed. It flashed across her mind that he had still not mentioned why he had come. There was no reason why he should, but just the same she could not help an illogical resentment that he should know her reason for being here, and yet keep her ignorant of his own.

'I'll forget him the moment I'm back at work,' she assured herself, but her assurance lacked conviction. 'All this is simply the result of accidental proximity, and having nothing much to do now Uncle's on the mend,' her mind persisted stubbornly. She had always scorned the girls who cried over holiday romances. They never came to anything. They were never meant to. They were born of brief summer freedom, sunny beaches, and time to play. Insubstantial, transient things, which faded like coloured rainbows the moment the holidays were over, so that by the time Christmas came around it was difficult to remember names to set to faces on the holiday snapshots.

'It's not like that this time,' her heart protested.

'It's got to be. It is with Nat,' she answered back in silent desperation. A sunny day, a casual kiss—they meant nothing to a man. And nothing to me, she tried to convince herself. 'It's simply a matter of chemistry.' Her scientifically trained mind knew that, beyond the shadow of a doubt. But the sweet, slumbering womanhood within her waited, and hoped, and she fell uneasily silent, and roused only when the great high sides of the tug loomed unexpectedly in front of the skiff, and Nat said,

'I want to collect another clip of films from my cabin.'

'It doesn't seem to occur to you that I might be in a hurry to go straight back home,' she retorted sharply, stung to anger because he had not bothered to ask her if she minded a diversion into the dock.

'But you're not in a hurry,' he stated calmly. 'Your aunt's having tea with her friend, so she won't be home until later.'

'You go, I'll stay here.' She sat stubbornly tight, as an idea struck her. If Nat left her alone in the skiff, she could start the outboard engine while he was on the tug, and head for home and leave him behind to his own devices. It would serve him right for foisting his company on her, and spoiling her afternoon. She did not know where he had left his car. Presumably outside Cliff House, since she had seen him watching her from the top of the cliffs, from where he must have begged a lift as far as the creek in the tradesman's van, which had been due to call at the house at about the time she left on her shell-gathering expedition. The thought of leaving Nat behind gave her immense satisfaction, and she gave a little triumphant wriggle on her seat. It would teach him a lesson if he had to walk from the harbour as far as Cliff House in order to pick up his car. He had been keen enough to teach her a lesson, she thought vindictively, so a taste of his own medicine would not be inappropriate.

'You go on,' she smiled up at him sweetly. 'I'll wait for you here.'

'I shan't be long.' He paused, struck by her sudden volte-face, and his eyes narrowed. 'On second thoughts, perhaps it would be better if you came along,' he decided shrewdly, and her brief moment of triumph evaporated.

'He's guessed!' She stared up at him, nonplussed. It was uncanny, as well as humiliating, the way he was able to read her thoughts.

'I shan't wander about the dock, if that's what's bothering you,' she snapped, grasping at the scattered remnants of her deception.

'I don't intend you to. Either of you,' he retorted evenly. He was jeering at her, she thought furiously, seeing through her subterfuge as easily as through a pane of clear glass. Telling her he knew, and daring her to deny it. With an easy movement he bent and picked up the dog, neatly putting an end to her plan.

'I'll carry Skip until we're on the tug.' He tucked the terrier under his arm and gained the dockside in one long stride.

'He knows I won't go home without Skip.'

Hot anger rose in her at the easy success of his counter-attack, and she got to her feet with a quick jump. What she intended to do she could not tell, and she was given no time to find out. Deprived of the counter-balance of Nat's weight, the boat tipped, and Dee's incautious movement rocked it further still. She flailed her arms wildly, trying to regain her balance, and grasped at the tiller for support. It proved an unwise leaning post. The moment her hand descended on the long wood her own weight swung it away from her, and helplessly she went with it, unable to let go, unable to help herself.

'Nat!' The cry was wrung from her as her head and shoulders faced their own reflection in the murky waters of the dock. 'Nat, help. . . .' Her face was within two inches of the rubbish-strewn water when,

'You're not even safe to be left on your own in the skiff.' He hooked impatient fingers inside her skirt band and hauled her ignominiously back into the boat. 'Now perhaps you'll stop arguing, and come with me.' With one arm—he still held the terrier under the other—he half pulled, half lifted her out of the skiff on to the blessedly unmoving surface of the dock, and still keeping his fingers round her wrist as if he did not trust her even now not to wander off among the cargo which the group of stevedores was handling further along the quay, he steered her firmly towards the gang plank leading on to the tug's deck. It was narrow, with no hand rail, and it bent in the middle. Dee looked down. The water was a long way below them, and scattered with a miscellany of debris from the activity on the dockside that made a possible ducking the reverse of inviting.

'I—can't walk up that!' She panicked, and her voice rose when Nat's grip on her did not slacken. 'I'm not going to walk up that,' she protested.

'You either walk up it yourself, or I'll carry you up.' The grim set of his jaw told her he meant it. 'It's perfectly safe,' he said impatiently, 'just walk in front of me. I've got hold of you, you can't possibly fall.' His fingers changed from her wrist back to the waistband of her skirt, and propelled her unwilling feet on to the plank.

'Now I know what it feels like to walk the plank!' Her attempt at humour failed dismally, and she wished she could share his conviction about her safety. She gulped as the springy wood bounced under her nervous steps. She glanced down, and the water looked a million miles away. So did the deck of the tug above them. Her feet froze in mid-step, and she longed to shut her eyes. Impulsively she reached behind her and clutched at Nat's hand with nervous fingers, envying the terrier its safe seat in his arms.

'Don't look down.' Nat spoke sharply, bringing her eyes

open again. 'The deck's just above you, it only needs a couple more steps.' He made her take the steps.

'He's got no feeling, no imagination,' she told herself furiously, unable to withstand the hard thrust in the middle of her back that forced her feet forward, upwards, and on to the deck of the tug. He loosed her then and she fumbled for her handkerchief, her palms clammy from fright, and tried not to miss the feel of his hand holding her.

'Now you've arrived, you might as well see the tug,' he said calmly. 'She's worth inspection.' He spoke with obvious pride, and she straightened, grasping at the opportunity to forget the means by which she had just arrived, and the unpalatable fact that she would have to depart by the same unstable route. The vessel looked even bigger from the deck than it had done from the shore. She gazed about her with unwilling interest, and something approaching awe. The tug was purpose-built, strong, impregnable. Like Nat. The thought flitted across her mind and she thrust it from her impatiently. But the rugged lines of the ship held a strange beauty of their own. It drew her against her will. Like Nat. . . .

'Is there anything I can get for you, Mr Archer?'

'No, thanks, George. I only came to get a film from my cabin. I'm still keeping a few in there, just for the moment,' Nat answered the burly, jerseyed figure who appeared from below. There did not seem to be anyone else on the vessel. Dee sensed an emptiness about the tug that she found strangely disconcerting. Its workmanlike appearance demanded the bustle of busy life, and the stillness was almost eerie. Perhaps the crew were on leave while the ship was in dock. Nat had left his films in his cabin 'just for the moment', which suggested he intended to remove them out of the way very soon. Perhaps because his cabin was going to be refitted.

'You can run free for a while,' he bent down and released the terrier on to its feet on the deck. 'There's not much mischief you can get into here,' he added.

'You spoke too soon!' Dee wailed. 'Why didn't you keep hold of him? Skip, come back!' There *was* someone else on the ship. Some*thing* else, to be exact. A sleek black cat followed the jerseyed man up the companionway and curled round his legs in an ingratiating manner, then stiffened and arched as it caught sight of the terrier. With a joyful bark the dog gave chase, but its quarry was on familiar ground, and within seconds it had ascended out of reach, and crouched, spitting obscenities at the frustrated dog from a spar overhead.

'Leave the dog alone.' To her amazement, instead of shouting at the terrier, Nat merely laughed, and reaching out he took hold of her arm, checking her move to grab Skip. 'It's every dog's right to chase cats,' he chuckled. 'You can't shout at him for obeying his instincts.'

He said it softly, deliberately rolling the words round his tongue, his black eyes boring into her own, and a rush of colour stained her throat and cheeks, deepening with anger and confusion as his dual meaning penetrated her consciousness.

A sunny day, a casual kiss, they meant nothing to a man.

'You can't shout at him for obeying his instincts.'

She *wanted* to shout at him, accuse him, condemn him for playing with her heart, for tossing it to and fro like a case ball to fill the idle hours with a casual game until the tug should be ready to put out to sea again and carry Nat away to other interests, other climes. Fresh fields for his talents—and his heart?—to conquer, with never a backward thought to the desolation he left behind, which was her own deflated heart, left stranded in the shallows of a hopeless yearning that would never know fulfilment, and never again know peace.

CHAPTER FIVE

'Come on, Skip, it's time to go.'

It annoyed her that the terrier obeyed him. With praiseworthy self sacrifice, the dog left the cat and came wagging towards Nat, its two front paws eager against his knees, begging to be picked up again.

'I'll carry him,' Dee began, and snapped her fingers to the dog, then she checked, and the breath stopped in her throat as she remembered how they had come aboard the tug, and the means by which they must inevitably leave it.

'See you, George,' Nat took casual leave of the jerseyed man. 'Contact me if there's anything you need.'

'Aye, I'll do that, Mr Archer.'

'Come on, Skip.' Nat pocketed his films, scooped up the dog, and stepped towards the gap in the guard rail. Instead of following him, Dee hung back. Her feet felt as if they were frozen to the spot.

'I can't go down that plank, not again!' she wailed. The thought of going down it was even worse than the memory of coming up. She risked a peep over the side of the tug, and her face went white. The slope seemed as steep as Everest, and the plank itself even narrower than she remembered it. Even in her tennis pumps she would never be able to obtain sufficient grip to remain upright.

'There isn't any other way ashore.' Nat turned at the rail and surveyed her impatiently. 'We can't swing you overboard in a net, we haven't got a crane working,' he jeered at her hesitation. 'And you can't stay on board—think of George's reputation,' he taunted. 'Come on, I'll hold you.' He reached out to catch her arm, and she flung his hand away violently, unable to control herself.

'I can't walk down that plank, I can't!' Her voice rose, and with a shudder she covered her face with her hands. 'I can't,' she whispered, and her voice broke.

'You really are scared, aren't you?' Nat paused and eyed her keenly. 'Why didn't you tell me you'd got no head for heights, before we came up?' he demanded sharply, blaming her for the difficulty. She raised her head and stared at him, incensed at the blame, but unable to stem the flood of fear that turned her dark blue eyes almost as black as Nat's own with apprehension. Nat had forced her to come on to the tug, she had not come of her own free will.

'How was I to know what it would be like?' she cried indignantly. She had never had to put her head for heights to the test before. Now she had found out, it was too late. 'Surely there must be some other way down?'

'Only if you slides down a rope, miss,' the man called George said practically. 'On tugs, we don't have gangways like the passenger liners do. We has to make do with things like planks.' He was honest, but it was neither help nor consolation to Dee in her present predicament.

'Take hold of the dog, will you?' Nat sounded resigned. He handed over Skip to the seaman, and before Dee realised what he was about to do, he stepped towards her and picked her up in his arms.

'Close your eyes and don't struggle,' he warned her, 'or we'll both land in the dock.'

She could not struggle if she tried. Her whole body felt stiff with fear, and she closed her eyes because she dared not look, as she felt Nat stride forward on to the plank. It sprung under his step, and with a convulsive movement she turned her face into his jersey. And penetrating her fear, she became aware of the strong, even beat of his heart under the softness of her cheek, the black silk of his jersey too fine to subdue the steady throb that even the burden of her weight did nothing to disturb. She could not say the same for her own palpitating member. It set up an answering, tremulous fluttering inside her breast that had nothing to do with heights or gangplanks, or the fear of a ducking, and everything to do with the feel of Nat's arms round her, holding her close against him, the feel of his heart beat against her cheek. It drove away the reason why he held her, and her fear, and left only a raw awareness of him that set her pulses hammering and stopped her breath in her throat. On an impulse she turned her head further still and pressed her lips against the spot where she felt his heart beat.

'You can open your eyes now, we're down.'

'Why don't gangplanks stretch for ever?' she wondered despairingly, and tried to subdue the stab of pure jealousy that pierced through her as Nat released her on to her feet, and immediately turned to take the terrier from the seaman's arms into his own as the man followed them surefootedly down the plank and on to the quayside.

'We'll have to fix up something a bit more secure for you, the next time you come aboard,' the burly seaman told her kindly, and Nat laughed.

'There won't be a next time,' he said casually, and Dee felt the sky go dark. He could not know how his words pierced her heart. The shaft of an archer found its mark, and through the gaping wound it left behind she felt as if her very life was draining away. With blurred eyes she turned on her heel and stumbled back towards the skiff.

'Stay on the quay for a minute.' Nat caught up with her, and swung down into the skiff first. He bent and put down the dog, then reached up to help her, but she hardly heard what he said, hardly even felt his hands hold her through the numb misery that strove to find an answer to the question,

'Does he mean there won't be a next time, because the tug will be gone? Or because he doesn't want to take me aboard, except to stop me from making off with the skiff and leaving him behind?'

The thought of making off with the skiff and leaving Nat stranded to walk back to his car appealed to her at the time, but the thought of Nat taking the tug, and himself, off into the unknown, and leaving her behind for ever, hurt unbearably, Dee discovered. It was one thing to face the possibility in theory, and quite another to face the prospect in stark reality. And what hurt most of all was the fact that Nat had not told her he was leaving, or when. He just capped the seaman's casual remark, and left her to infer what she liked from both. He did not think it worth while telling her, explaining to her.

'If he wants to be secretive, let him,' she muttered rebelliously, deliberately whipping up her resentment, using anger as a shield to protect her from the hurt. 'I don't care,' she told herself, and kept on repeating it, until by the time Nat beached the skiff and they waded ashore together, and she had put the roll of cotton wool containing the shells into the safety of the string bag, refusing to allow him to carry it for her, she really believed she did not care, and her new independence allowed her to scramble without his help up the cliff, albeit by the easier route. She pulled herself up the steeper bits by dint of grasping the heather roots, glad of the physical challenge to still her mind and stop her from remembering that Nat climbed just behind her, within arm's reach of her. She kept her eyes on Skip instead, using the dog as a moving anchor for her thoughts, that once her attention wandered away she knew would return to Nat, and start hurting all over again.

The red van was parked outside the gateway to Cliff House. He must have felt very sure of himself, very sure of her, she thought resentfully, to so casually abandon his vehicle and ride umpteen miles to the other side of the headland in the tradesman's van, in order to take one photograph, and depend on herself to bring him back in the skiff. His very confidence that she would fall in meekly with his plan turned her manufactured resentment into reality, and she frowned.

'I'll take the shells indoors while you start your van.' She turned her back and started to walk towards the garden gate. 'I won't invite him in,' she determined inhospitably. She would show him that he could not take her for granted, use her to further his own ends as and when he pleased.

'Hold on to Skip's collar, never mind the shells,' he ordered her brusquely. Disconcertingly, he did not seem to even notice her lack of hospitality, and his indifference piqued her as much as his order annoyed her.

'Skip will be safe enough, once he's inside the gate,' she replied shortly, and deliberately drew her fingers back from reaching for the dog's collar. 'It's high time Nat learned I'm not here simply to obey his orders,' she fumed silently. 'Come on, into the garden,' she shooed the terrier through and shut the wicket gate behind them with a sharp slam, leaving Nat on the other side. She felt strongly tempted to walk straight on along the garden path and ignore Nat's leavetaking, she even took a step or two away from the gate, with the terrier obediently trotting towards the front door of the house ahead of her.

The van engine started, and she noticed the gap in the fence at the same time.

'Skip. . . .' she warned quickly, and the dog hesitated, and looked back. 'He's learned his lesson,' Dee breathed thankfully, and then Nat revved his engine into reverse. If he had been driving the Rover it probably would not have had the same effect. The quiet, well-bred purr of the big engine might not have tipped the scales in quite such a devastating manner as the small, fast revving engine achieved. It exploded into noisy life, and,

'Skip, come back!' The terrier evidently knew the gaps in the fence better than Dee did. Probably he was responsible for them in the first place. Whatever the reason, the dog scampered for the nearest gap with unerring accuracy, and a speed which Dee could not hope to match, his recently acquired good behaviour thrown to the winds in the joy of the chase.

Nat had no hope of seeing the terrier in time. Skip leapt through the gap in the fence and made straight for the rear of the reversing vehicle, on the blind side from the driver, snapping at the turning wheels.

'Nat, stop! Stop!'

He reacted with a speed that awed her, even in the midst of her distress. At her first scream he slammed on his brake, but even so his back bumper caught the little dog a glancing blow that bowled it head over heels into the tangled grass of the verge.

'Why didn't you look where you were going?' Dee panted to a halt beside the van.

'Why didn't you hold on to him, like I told you to?' He was out of his seat in a flash, confronting her, his black brows drawn together, and his face dark with anger. 'If you'd done as I told you in the first place, it would never have happened,' he accused her.

'I. . . .'

'Never mind making excuses now,' he cut her short abruptly. 'Where's Skip?' He looked round, unable to find the dog immediately, then the terrier whined, answering for her, trying valiantly to struggle to its feet when it heard its name spoken. Nat spun on his heel, turning his back on Dee, and with one quick stride he reached the grass verge and bent over the dog. She followed him, her feet dragging, her legs shaking so much that she could scarcely walk. She hardly dared to look at the terrier, but she crouched beside it just the same, beside Nat, her hands reaching out to comfort and reassure, where she could find no reassurance or comfort for herself. She hated Nat for what had happened, for blaming her, she told herself fiercely, and felt she hated him even more, because she blamed herself.

'Is he . . .?' The lump in her throat made it impossible for her to go on.

'I don't think anything's broken.' His slim brown fingers did not pause in their gentle exploration, and his tone changed as he spoke encouragingly to the terrier, so that in the midst of its shock and pain the small tail wagged in answer. His voice hardened again when he spoke to Dee.

'We'll take him to the vet, just to be on the safe side.' Cautiously he rose to his feet, lifting the terrier with him, careful to make no sudden move that might jolt Skip and cause him further pain. 'Go and sit in the passenger seat of the van,' he told Dee curtly. 'I'll lie Skip across your lap, he'll ride more easily that way.'

'I can't pull the door open. The lock jams on that side.' She remembered when Nat let her out of the van before, he had had to wrench at the door handle with all his strength to get it to open, a strength that her own trembling hands could not possibly match.

'The door opens easily enough now, the lock's been replaced.' His eyes hardened to match his voice, accusing her of making excuses, of being afraid to face the emergency, and her own responsibility for it.

'It's not true,' she longed to cry out, to throw his unspoken accusation back in his face. Instead she turned in silence and fumbled at the door handle, reduced to speechlessness because she was, desperately, afraid for Skip. And in his present mood, she was more than a little afraid of Nat.

The door opened easily enough, as he predicted it would, and she wriggled into the passenger seat and made as flat a lap as possible, all the time avoiding Nat's look because she sensed the contempt in his eyes, and could not meet it. He bent and eased the terrier flat across her knees.

'Skip, I'm sorry,' she whispered, leaning her face down to meet the dog's forgiving tongue as Nat shut the door on her, and strode round to his side of the van.

'Don't cuddle him.' He slid behind the wheel and spoke to Dee sharply. 'If there's a bone broken, it'll only make things worse.'

'But you said there wasn't?'

'I said I didn't *think* there was,' he corrected her bluntly. 'Until he's been X-rayed, we can't be sure, and it's best to handle him as little as possible in the meantime.'

'There's nothing broken.' An endless hour later the white-coated vet released Dee from a purgatory of worry. 'He's bruised a bit, but it's nothing serious. He'll be stiff for a day or two, maybe have a bit of a limp, but that's all. It'll soon wear off.' He gave the terrier into her eager arms. 'Don't spoil him,' he smiled, wise in the ways of pets and their owners. 'If you do he'll only play up to it, and make his limp last twice as long. How did it happen?' he enquired of Nat.

'He was chasing my van,' he replied shortly.

'In that case, let's hope he's learned his lesson,' the vet replied drily.

'Let's hope it's taught you one, too,' Nat growled to Dee as they quit the surgery together, and she bridled, her sturdy independence reasserting itself on her release from tension.

'I suppose you mean you hope it'll teach me to obey your orders the very second they're uttered,' she flashed back at him angrily. 'The crew on your tug might have to, because you employ them. But I'm not one of them, thank goodness,' she added bitingly. 'I don't have to do as you say, and I've got no intention of starting,' she told him forthrightly. All men were arrogant, but Nat Archer was impossible, she seethed inwardly, and sought for excuses on the way back to Cliff House for sending him on his way without inviting him into the house. She had succeeded before, but Skip was now paying the price, her conscience reminded her, and remorse for the consequences was sufficient to make her allow Nat to pick up the dog in his arms and accompany her up the garden path without outward protest. The front door of the house was open, and voices sounded from inside.

'It sounds as if Aunt Martha and Helen are home.'

'Whatever happened?' The two elderly women viewed their appearance with consternation, that changed to relief as they related their story, and ended with the vet's verdict. 'Pop Skip in his basket,' her aunt indicated the comfortable wicker bed, well padded with a clean blanket, and Nat lowered his burden carefully on to it.

'We'll put him on a running lead for a day or two,' Martha Lawrence decided. 'By the time he's got over his fright and is ready to get into mischief again, your uncle will be home to control him,' she said thankfully.

'When?' Dee's face lit up. She had not really felt the burden of her responsibilities to her uncle's household until this afternoon. Now, quite suddenly, she felt them to be onerous. If her uncle had been at home, Skip would not have been hurt. She would not have been hurt, because she would not have met Nat. 'Once Uncle's back home, Nat won't have any excuse to call at Cliff House again,' she told herself, and tried without success to feel glad. Perversely, her spirits dropped to zero at the thought, so that she scarcely heard her aunt reply.

'In ten days, the doctor said.'

'That means he'll still have to endure another Friday with fish fingers for lunch,' Helen laughed. 'Poor Frank, it's no fare to put before a fisherman,' she sympathised.

'It'll make him appreciate my cooking all the more when he does return home,' the fisherman's wife chuckled. 'By the way, Helen, I don't think you've met Nat Archer? He's Wordesley Archer's youngest son,' she performed belated introductions.

'The black sheep of the family,' Dee muttered maliciously. Nat glanced across at her sharply as he shook hands with Helen, and she had the satisfaction of knowing that her remark had registered. 'At least that's evened the score a bit,' she told herself with unrepentant glee.

'Nat owns the big sea-going tug that's tied up in the harbour,' her aunt went on, happily unaware of the cross-currents of antagonism that flowed around her. 'He tows the tankers and the big ships when they break down at sea, and so on,' she waved an all-inclusive hand.

'They must be very grateful for your help,' Helen smiled as she shook hands. She was a beautician, and had not the vaguest notion of maritime matters, but there was no mistaking the approval in her eyes as they rested upon Nat.

'He seems to have cast a spell on Helen, as well as on Aunt Martha.' Dee glowered at the innocent pair as Nat responded.

'The ships' crews are probably relieved to see us when they're in trouble, but I doubt if they're exactly grateful for our help,' he laughed, and taking pity on Helen's obvious puzzlement he added, 'the moment we put a line aboard a stranded vessel, we claim salvage money. The tug has to pay for itself,' he said simply. 'That's how it makes its living.'

'It's all much too complicated for me,' Helen smiled, and added with a glance at her watch, 'Well, I must be off. I hope to see you again soon, Mr Archer, and you can tell me more about your tug. In the meantime, I've got a client waiting.' She turned back to Dee's aunt. 'I'll pick you up again tomorrow,' she promised, 'and Dee can take you on Friday when she collects her car.'

'My car's being repaired,' Dee began.

'The garage rang just after you went out this morning,' her aunt brought her up to date. 'I forgot to tell you when you came in with Skip just now—the foreman said your car should be ready to collect by Friday morning.'

Which meant if she could obtain some fresh fish the day before, she could take it into the hospital on Friday morning and rescue her uncle from the possibility of consuming another plateful of fish fingers. The happy thought struck Dee. She nearly uttered it out loud, and managed to check herself just in time. Nat had heard her say she intended to go shell gathering, and he followed her to the creek. She did not intend him to follow her on to the fishing grounds as well. Or—another thought occurred to rasp her already sensitive nerves on that score—or possibly try to prevent her from taking the smack out fishing at all.

'He shan't stop me,' she vowed, and decided not to say anything to her aunt and Helen about her plans, either. They were just as likely to comment to Nat if they bumped into him. Not that there was any reason for him to come to Cliff House again, now Helen had volunteered to take her aunt into the hospital on the following day, and her own car would be ready after that. A wave of desolation took hold of her at the thought that Nat would no longer need to call, and she thrust it aside impatiently.

'I'll be able to manage the fishing smack better than the skiff, the engine's got a self-starter, and it's just a matter of steering it in the right direction after that.' Bending her mind to practical matters prevented her from thinking about Nat, and she laid her plans for the next day with meticulous care.

She knew whereabouts she could find plaice, she had accompanied her uncle on long-line fishing expeditions in the smack more than once, and knew the area he usually made for. If she went to roughly the same spot she saw no reason why she should not catch all the fish she wanted, and be back at home before her aunt returned in the evening. It all seemed quite simple and straightforward.

'You can stay at home this time, and guard the house.' She made it simpler still by refusing Skip's eager entreaties to come with her. The little dog showed hardly any signs of his ordeal of the day before, but she hardened her heart. She did not feel equal to coping with any more complications, she told herself firmly. Particularly if Nat was not going to be around to help her? 'I don't want him around!' she exploded fiercely, and grabbing her anorak she made for the harbour before her mind could pose any more unwanted questions.

'Your uncle's smack's all fuelled up and ready for off, Miss Lawrence.' One of the men from her uncle's fleet was busy about his own boat moored close by, and he greeted her with a cheerful wave as she reached the harbour. 'Will you want anyone to crew for you?'

'No, thanks, Hugh. I'm only going to drop a line over the side in the hope of catching a few plaice,' she explained the reason for her intention. 'I'll bait a dozen or so hooks, and leave it at that for today.' She grimaced. Baiting hooks was not her favourite occupation. Her uncle usually did it for her. In spite of her lip service to Women's Liberation, Dee still had a few reservations about which jobs belonged to men and which jobs belonged to women. Baiting hooks, to her way of thinking, lay squarely in the former category.

'I'll bait you a line.' The skipper named Hugh grinned at her expression, and obligingly left his own work to save her from the unwelcome task. 'Don't go out too far,' he advised her when it was done. 'There's a report of a blow on the way,' he explained laconically.

'I'd thought of going out as far as the Whale,' Dee mentioned the long, fish-shaped mudbank lying south of the harbour bar, which lay partly exposed when the tide was at its lowest. There would be nothing of it showing now because the tide had already started to turn, coming in, but the bell-buoy that marked it would be sufficient to guide her, she judged. 'Uncle Frank usually fishes just beyond that point when he's only using the lines.'

'Aye, you should get what you want from around there, and it's not too far out,' the seaman agreed, and returned to his tasks on his own boat, evidently satisfied that Dee was not about to disappear for good over the horizon. She boarded her uncle's smack with a sigh of relief that she could do so by the simple expedient of lowering herself off the harbour steps, instead of negotiating a plank to get on board. 'Hugh's nice, but he's fussing unnecessarily,' she decided, with a glance at the clear sky, and turned her attention to the engine. She had taken over the wheel of the smack several times before, so the steering presented her with no problems, and her years of driving her own car made the simple controls child's play. The engine obligingly started at the first try, and her lips gave a small, triumphant upward tilt.

'I'm going to enjoy this afternoon,' she discovered unexpectedly, and turned her attention to negotiating a safe passage among the miscellany of small craft busily plying to and fro across the sunlit water. It was hot in the glass enclosure of the wheelhouse, and she slid the window open, letting in the low-pitched moan of the dredger that made a daily background noise as it worked in the harbour, its presence warning the initiated why nothing much larger than a cargo vessel should venture into the harbour as it fought its endless battle against the silt which posed a constant threat to the valuable working depth of the water.

Nat's tug still lay at anchor at the Archer quay; Dee could see the tall lines of it but—she squinted backwards through the rear window of the wheelhouse—there was no sign of life aboard. She shrugged, relieved, and at the same time oddly disappointed. If Nat had been aboard, she would have enjoyed the knowledge that she was even now slipping out of the harbour under his very nose, observed, but unrecognised. She felt positive he would not be able to identify which was her uncle's personal vessel out of the inshore fleet, and—an impish grin tugged at the corners of her mouth—he would not be able to see whether it was a man or a woman at the wheel. She acknowledged to herself now why she had put on a navy blue sweater and navy slacks to come out in, disguising herself in the standard fisherman's garb.

Secure in the knowledge that she was safe from recognition, she pointed the nose of the smack out towards the harbour bar. Its arm closed round the small haven, secure and sheltering. At least, that was the way in which Dee had always regarded it. Just lately, she discovered to her dismay, it had taken on the aspect more of a prison wall than a haven, stifling, closing her in.

'I'm lucky to be able to spend the summer months at the seaside,' she tried to scold herself into a more reasonable frame of mind. 'And anyway, it's not for much longer now.' The sun lost a little of its brightness at the thought that it was not for much longer, and she gave herself a mental shake. 'Concentrate on catching fish,' she told herself sternly. 'That's the only important thing at the moment.' She used immediate necessities as a shield against the self-inflicted wounds of her own thoughts, and felt a surge of relief when the monotonous tolling of the bell-buoy impinged on her consciousness, and forced her to give her whole attention to her whereabouts.

'Slow down, veer round the end of the mudbank, and fish from the seaward side.' Dee repeated the instructions she had heard many times from her uncle when he handed over the wheel to her keeping while he baited his lines, and she carefully steered the smack round the end of the whale-shaped bank, keeping well clear of the fringes of it for fear of fouling the propeller, until she judged it was safe to turn about and run parallel with the bank on its seaward side.

The tide was coming in fast now. Beyond the comparative shelter of the bank the run of the water was much stronger, making itself felt in the increased motion of the fishing smack. The wind, too, had freshened since the morning. Dee stuck her head through the open wheelhouse window and gasped as it blew her hair across her eyes and her breath back into her nostrils.

'Thank goodness I brought an anorak!' She slammed the window shut and reached for her windproof. It was cooler on the water than she had bargained for. With a quick flick she killed the engine and hurried forward.

'Perhaps Hugh was right about a storm coming, after all.' Out of the shelter of the wheelhouse, the wind was decidedly rough, to the extent that it was already beginning to drive the water. Small patches of white cloud broke away from the mass gathering on the horizon, and came scudding overhead, giving a clear indication of the wind speed, and Dee watched them for a moment with a frown.

'I won't stay out for long,' she compromised. 'I'll make do with the for'ard anchor for today.' Her uncle usually used two anchors when he fished near the mudbank, one forward and one aft. Steadiers, he called them, and Dee assumed their use was to prevent the boat from drifting back on to his fishing lines.

'If Hugh's "blow" is going to amount to anything, I'd better be back in harbour before it starts,' she grimaced at the hurrying clouds. 'Down you go!' She released the forward anchor. 'I won't bother with the other. I'll fish for'ard, then any drift will have to be away from the anchor, and it'll keep my line clear. I hope I catch something, now I've gone to all this trouble.' She sent her line overboard to follow the anchor.

That done, she crouched in the shelter of the wheelhouse and settled down to wait. It was warm out of the wind. The sun shone, and the boat rocked. After a while the rocking grew less, until it almost ceased altogether.

'The tide must have stopped running,' Dee diagnosed drowsily. She did not bother to look at her watch. She knew roughly the times of the tides, but not with any great exactitude. There was always sufficient depth of water in the harbour to take the fishing smack, even at the lowest ebb, so it was of no consequence.

She supposed she must have fallen asleep. She could not be sure. She denied the accusation strenuously afterwards to Nat, but when she last looked round her she had the sea to herself. She blinked her eyes open and stared at the massive lines of the tug that had not been there, surely only minutes before? It stood off from her some distance, but its immense size made it seem to tower over the fishing smack. Made the figure on the bridge seem to tower over her.

'Dee!'

She gained her feet in a startled jump as her name boomed across the water.

'Dee, wake up!'

Nat stood on the bridge of the tug, his black slacks and black rollneck sweater making a commanding silhouette, and he used the loudhailer in his hand to telling effect.

'Dee, for heaven's sake, wake up. . . .'

'I'm not asleep,' she denied angrily. Even as she shouted back at him, she realised how useless it was. Her cry was puny competition for the waves, and the whine of the wind. A chill went through her as she realised how much the wind had gained in force. But she shouted just the same. Black fury made her raise her voice and throw it back at Nat across the water. How dared he bawl at her through a loudhailer? she seethed. The fact that his voice would not have reached her across the distance without it was beside the point. He had no right to shout at her at all. The sense of what he shouted did not begin to penetrate for a minute or two, until she became aware of other figures active on the deck of the tug, and realised they were in the process of launching a small boat over the side.

It reached the water with the brisk efficiency of frequent practice, and—she stared in startled wonderment—Nat followed it by the simple process of sliding down the rope that tethered it to the tug's side. For a second her hands flew to her throat, then she let out a sigh of relief as he landed easily, and immediately turned and bent down. The splutter of an outboard motor came across the water, and he straightened again, casting off the rope, and her qualms returned as the light skiff reared and dipped like a cockleshell on the wilding sea, making directly towards the fishing smack. She leaned over the rail and watched its progress, her heart in her mouth, and the knuckles of her hands gleaming white with the force of her grip. They whitened further still as Nat came in line below her, and raising his face he shouted.

'Stand clear of the rail!'

He did not need the loudhailer this time to make himself understood. His voice carried clearly upwards, and her face went as white as her knuckles at his curt command.

'I'll do no such thing!' she shouted back at him angrily. Why should she? she fumed. The fishing smack was not his boat. He was not the skipper, and she was not a member of his crew to be galvanised into action the moment he barked an order.

'Do as I say, I've no time to argue.' His upraised face carried the same clear warning of impending storm as the rapidly darkening sky, and for a second Dee's courage failed her. Her hands lost their grip on the rail, and she took an involuntary step backwards as Nat shouted up grimly,

'I'm coming aboard!'

CHAPTER SIX

HE already *was* aboard.

With breathtaking speed, and devastating success, Nat had stormed her defences like the pirates of old, enslaving her heart and capturing her mind, yet leaving his own buccaneering spirit to range as free as the sea wind after which he had named his tug, she thought bitterly, to live and love again when the restless breeze of adventure turned and took him away, and out of her life.

'Stand clear!' he repeated his warning.

'If only I had in the first place,' Dee moaned softly, hopelessly. But regret was a fruitless emotion for a captive already bound by unbreakable chains.

She jumped violently as metal glinted in mid-air, arcing towards her before it descended with excellent aim and a loud clatter on to the rail of the smack close beside her. The rope attached to the grappling hook went taut as Nat gave it an experimental tug, which must have satisfied him that it would hold, because he immediately began to climb. She stared down at him with angry bewilderment. The agile, black-clad figure, shinning up the boarding rope, the looming tug, the heaving sea.... It did not take much to imagine a cutlass between his teeth, she thought half hysterically.

'Why the dramatics?' She swung to face him and spoke sharply as he vaulted over the side of the rail and landed surefooted on the deck beside her.

'I've got to get you off here before this blow gets any worse,' he answered her curtly.

'I can get myself off, whatever that means,' she retorted with spirit. Off what, she had no idea. Presumably he meant off the fishing ground. The thought reminded her of her line, and the reason why she had come in the first place.

'The minute I've pulled in my line, I intend to go back anyway,' she told him.

'Never mind your line ... oh well, I suppose an extra couple of minutes can't do any more damage,' he growled, and with the speed of exasperation he grasped the fishing line from out of her fingers and pulled it in hand over hand with a swiftness and sureness that spoke of much practice.

'I've caught a plaice! Oh, look and another one!' Dee could not hide her elation at the success of her fishing expedition, not even in the face of Nat's grim-visaged lack of comment. 'It was worth coming out for, after all. Uncle Frank won't have to have fish fingers for his last Friday in hospital. He'll be delighted....'

'I doubt he'll be either delighted, or think his fresh plaice is worth what this trip's likely to cost him.' Nat deftly unhooked the wriggling fish, and Dee turned her back and looked the other way, squeamishly thankful on this one point at least that Nat was there to do the job for her. Unhooking struggling fish was even worse than baiting hooks in the first place.

'Leave them in the boxes.' He tossed the plaice into the two containers she had brought in readiness, and turned abruptly towards the wheelhouse. 'I want to see if the smack will get under way by herself.'

'The engine works perfectly well. It started first go when I set out.' Dee's chin tilted proudly, her competence questioned. 'I'm quite capable of taking the boat back on my own.' She ducked under his arm as he opened the wheelhouse door, and spun round on him furiously when she felt his fingers close round her wrist, holding her back from touching the controls. 'Loose me!' she demanded, and her voice rose.

'Not until I've taken a look aft first.' His single glance

at the controls seemed to give him whatever information he sought, and he turned about, pulling her with him.

'If you want to stand and admire the scenery, you can do that from the deck of your own tug,' she cried sarcastically. 'I want to go home!' Suddenly she wished she had never left it. Coping with Skip's antics was a thousand times easier than coping with Nat. She twisted her arm violently, attempting to loosen his hold, but the only effect was for his fingers to tighten their grip in a way that made her wince.

'You're hurting me!' she cried angrily.

'Not half as much as you might get hurt if you have to sit out a storm stranded on this mudbank,' he growled back unsympathetically.

'I'm nowhere near the mudbank!'

'No?' He flicked her a look that questioned her reason as well as her seamanship. 'Come and have a look.' With a set jaw he tugged her close to the rail. 'Look overboard,' he commanded, in a tone that suggested he felt strongly tempted to drop her in the direction he was looking, and against her better judgment her eyes followed where he pointed.

'There's nothing there except....'

'Except mud,' he finished for her cuttingly.

'It's well covered with water.' She stopped. It should not have been there at all; the smack should have been well clear of the mudbank. She swallowed hard.

'I suppose you didn't think it was necessary to put out a stern anchor?' His voice was the unforgiving one of a seaman finding a good ship grounded because of an amateur's carelessness.

'I thought ... I meant....' Realisation of the reason for the two anchors dawned upon Dee at the same time as the consequences of her action broke over her in a cold wave. 'I thought the for'ard anchor would hold the smack clear of the mudbank.'

'So it might have done, in a flat calm,' Nat broke in impatiently. 'But you can hardly apply that description to the sea that's running now,' he flung an angry hand towards the swift flow of the tide.

'I wasn't to know,' Dee defended herself hotly against the biting criticism in his voice, in his expression. 'I'm not a seaman.'

'The same applies here as it did on the docks.' He still had not forgiven her for her faux pas with the flour sack, and he gave her no quarter now. 'Even a landlubber should be capable of using common sense,' he threw at her contemptuously, and she flushed, but before she could speak he went on remorselessly.

'The tide's coming in fast, and the wind's driving it. Either is more than sufficient to move the smack, and your one anchor merely acted as a tether to swing the stern in a half circle, straight on to the one thing you should have avoided at all costs.'

'I can see that for myself, without needing a lecture from you,' she flared, goaded into fury by his overbearing attitude. Why did it have to be Nat who appeared on the scene? she wondered wrathfully. Why could it not have been Hugh? The kindly, elderly fishing skipper, who would have known how to cope with the emergency with no fuss, and less censure than the grim-faced, black-browed master of the tug? Her chin came up proudly, and she faced his hostility with a fiery spirit that for a moment brought a gleam deep into the man's eyes, but she was too incensed to be capable of interpreting stray gleams, and the next moment it disappeared as she said cuttingly,

'Instead of wasting time shouting at me, surely it's more important to get the smack free of the mudbank first, and hold an inquest on who's to blame afterwards?'

'There's no doubt who's to blame,' he thrust back uncompromisingly.

'All right, I admit it—I'm to blame. Now are you satisfied?' she shouted at him furiously. 'Now I'm going to start the engine and get the boat under way.' She spun away from him. 'There's enough time wasted already, arguing with you.' She never seemed to do anything else, when she was with Nat, she thought miserably. They seemed to act on one another like a torch to tinder.

'You're not to start the engine.'

'You can't stop me!' She faced him again, her eyes flashing.

'I can, and I will.' With the same deceptive lack of speed that had confused her before he reached out and caught her arm: She tried to duck away, but the ship's rail was at her back, and the only escape was overboard into the water.

'Let me go!' she demanded angrily.

'Not until you've listened to me.'

It was pointless, as well as undignified, to struggle. His strength was twice that of her own, and the anger that rode him made him invincible. Dee drew a deep breath, and with an immense effort forced herself to remain calm, to stand still, and say in as reasoning a voice as she could manage,

'The boat *can't* be embedded in the mud all that deeply, I haven't been at the fishing ground for long enough. A quick spurt with the engine should be enough to pull her clear. The mud's soft, so it won't damage the propeller.'

'It's obvious you don't know anything about mudbanks.'

'But. . . .'

'If the prop spun,' Nat silenced her and went on, 'it would probably only succeed in digging you even deeper into the bank than you are now, and make it harder than ever to force the mud to release you.'

'Force the mud to do what?' He was talking in riddles, and she had neither the time nor the patience to unravel them. She turned with a frown to tell him so, but he spoke first.

'Mud creates a suction.' His words came out clipped, economical, and with the tightly controlled patience of a tutor explaining a point for the umpteenth time to a particularly obtuse pupil. 'Anything that digs the stern deeper into the bank would only increase the suction, and make it more difficult to pull the smack clear without damage. And if the prop happened to catch on submerged debris, it could well be smashed beyond repair,' he added with brutal frankness. 'It's something I'm not prepared to risk.'

'It isn't your boat to risk, so it's not your decision,' she flashed back, resenting his command of the situation. 'He behaves as if he's on the bridge of his own tug, shouting orders at his crew,' she thought angrily.

'Perhaps you'd rather I left the smack, and you, to your own devices?' he suggested silkily, and there was steel in his eyes as well as his voice as he said it. 'There's a storm coming, and you shouldn't need telling what sort of performance the weather in these parts is capable of.' His eyes narrowed, watching her. Reading the doubt and the indecision, and, though she tried valiantly to hide it, the dawning terror in her eyes at the thought of being left stranded on the mudbank in the middle of a storm. Even during the summer, the coastal area around Penzyn could produce some of the worst weather conditions in the shortest time of any seaboard in the country, and she could not control a shiver.

'That settles it.' Nat saw the shiver, and knew it was not because she felt cold. 'I'll run a line aboard from the tug. There's an even chance that one good heave will pull the smack free without doing too much damage.'

Maybe the smack would escape its adventure without

damage. Her uncle's insurance policy most certainly would not.

'The moment we put a line aboard a stranded vessel, we claim salvage money.' Nat's words to Helen rang in her ears like a knell.

'You mustn't put a line aboard the smack,' she protested, and her voice rose with alarm. 'I won't allow you to.' She grasped desperately at the remnants of her departing courage, and faced him like a tigress defending her young. 'You'll claim salvage if you do. . . .'

The words were out before she could stop them. She had not meant to bare her fears so openly. She hated Nat for making her lose her pride in such a humiliating way. For a brief, awful moment she felt she would rather risk losing the smack than lower her pride before him.

'So it's the salvage that's worrying you.' His eyes watched her, noting her every reaction. 'If you hire a contractor, you must expect to pay,' he pointed out drily.

'I didn't hire you,' she flared, and her voice broke, perilously close to tears. She blinked them back impatiently. It would be the last straw if she were to cry in front of Nat. 'I didn't ask you to come,' she denied her need of him. But now he was here, and her traitorous heart refused to allow her to deny that it wanted him to stay. The harder she tried to convince herself that she wanted him to go, preferably out of her life for ever, the louder her heart protested at the thought. Nat had stormed over her defences and taken her heart as his booty, and without it she felt empty, stranded, like the smack was stranded, trapped in the shallows of longing that were rapidly becoming submerged in an ever deepening tide of despair.

'You only came out because you saw the chance of earning salvage money,' she accused him wildly. 'You must have seen what was happening, and you just sat there quietly and waited, knowing what the outcome would be.' She knew that was not true. She knew, with the wisdom of hindsight, just when the smack had gone aground, and the tug had been nowhere in sight at the time. She remembered the gradual cessation of movement just before she dozed off to sleep, remembered thinking the tide had stopped running. Now she knew it must have been when the stern ran aground, firming itself in the mudbank, and she had allowed herself to drop into sleep, lulled into a false sense of security by the very lack of movement that should have alerted her to the danger she was in. Bitter self-recrimination at her own carelessness stung her into attacking Nat.

'Tugs are nothing but sea vultures!' she flung at him stormily. 'They sit on the sidelines waiting for something to happen, and then when it does they close in on a crippled ship and make a feast of the remains.'

Her barb found its mark. His face went white with a harshly bridled fury that turned his eyes into burning coals, and his jaw into solid rock. Dee drew a quick breath, and the thrill of fear that coursed through her had nothing to do with the elements.

'If you must know, I don't intend to claim salvage money from your uncle,' he gritted through set teeth, and she let out her breath in a small sigh, only to draw it back again with a gasp as he went on tautly.

'I'll waive my claim for the fishing smack. But since I'll be salvaging the crew as well as the vessel,' his eyes bored into her own, holding her, rooting her to the spot, because she was the only crew the smack boasted, so he must mean herself, 'since I'll be salvaging the crew as well as the vessel, I'll take my payment direct from you instead.'

The only consolation Dee had was that the wheelhouse was between herself and the men on the tug. It offered kindly shelter to her pride, if nothing else. Nat showed her no mercy. With deadly expertise he exacted his payment to the last trembling ounce. His anger fused his kisses with the wrath of a lightning flash, burning her lips, her eyes, her throat, leaving a trail of fire across her cheeks. She struggled, but the combined strength of his hold, and her own heart's urgent longing, proved too much for her relatively puny defences, and at last her fists ceased their hopeless beating against his chest, and with a tiny moan of submission she surrendered to his arms, raised her face to let the lightning do its worst, fearing its power, and at the same time dreading that it might cease.

'Nat . . . Nat. . . .' she whispered.

'That will do on account,' he grated savagely, and taking her hands that were seeking to lock themselves behind his neck, he thrust her from him and ordered harshly,

'Stand where you are, and don't move. I'm going to signal to the tug to send across a line.'

It must have been fired from a gun of some sort, she supposed dully. In response to his wave a line came snaking through the air towards the fishing smack. It hit the deck with a sharp thud and started to slide back towards the rail, but Nat was there before it, capturing it with deft hands that immediately made it fast, and straight away turned to draw up the anchor. Dee felt as if he was drawing up the very anchor of her life along with it, leaving her to drift helplessly on a tide that ebbed and flowed between love and loathing in a way that left her mind bewildered, and near to despair.

'Throw out a line and anchor yourself to Nat,' her heart begged, in no doubt of the remedy.

'He wouldn't catch it if I did. He'd only let it fall back and sink.' And she would sink along with it, her mind answered her wretchedly.

'Hold tight, the tug's getting under way!'

Nat reached out and pulled her unceremoniously along with him into the confines of the wheelhouse as the tug started to draw away from them. Its movement was almost imperceptible at first, noticeable only by the action of the rope. The slack of it rose slowly out of the water, cascading bright drops as it gradually straightened until it finally snapped taut, and Dee felt the fishing smack shudder. Her hands flew to her throat. Would it pull the smack clear? Or would the mudbank, the locally notorious Whale, claim yet another victim to add to the long list of hapless vessels that over the years had become trapped and eventually broken up in its fearsome grip? If it did—she swallowed hard—it would be her fault, the result of her own ignorance, that Nat would undoubtedly call carelessness. Her eyes flew to his face, seeking reassurance, but his gaze was intent on the tug, the rope, the mudbank, waiting for the final heave that would pull them clear—or snap the rope.

She stared, fascinated, as the hawser stretched thin with the strain. 'Twanging tight' she had heard the local tugmen describe such ultimate tension. Surely it could not continue to withstand such a strain, and still refuse to break? Her nerves stretched along with the rope, as near to breaking point as must be the thin strand stretching between the two vessels, that was all that stood between her uncle's fishing smack and disaster.

'Hold tight, we're moving!'

Although she was expecting it, waiting for it, Dee was unprepared when the smack finally came free. With a loud, evil, sucking squelch the mud gave up its victim, with a suddenness that shot the smack like a cork from a bottle. The little fishing vessel gave a convulsive leap forward, and Dee's feet left the deck and she landed against Nat in a helpless tangle of arms and legs.

'I told you to hold tight.' He caught her, sorted her out, stood her upright, then held her against him with a hard arm.

'We're free!' she cried exultantly, forgetful of his earlier anger, forgetful of everything except that the smack was saved. It was too late to save herself. She was bound to Nat with unbreakable bonds, that might chafe her, and against which she might struggle, but for the rest of her life would hold her fast. But even these, for the moment, could not curb her elation at the smack's escape. Impulsively she hugged him, and felt a sharp pain pierce through her because he did not respond, while the lurching deck gradually steadied, and the familiar roll and dip of the normal, wave-induced motion reasserted itself, and he loosed his arms from around her, putting her from him.

'We still don't know if the prop's been damaged.' He poured cold water on her excitement, and she stared up at him, the elation draining from her face. 'The prop might have caught on some submerged wreckage. There's enough ships broken up on this mudbank to fill it with scrap metal, any bit of which could have bent the prop beyond repair,' he went on remorselessly. She nearly asked him,

'What prop?'

Any damage that might have been inflicted on the ship's mechanism was as nothing to the damage Nat had wreaked on her own motivating power, she thought unhappily. Gone was the alert, self-assured research chemist, confident in past years of training and experience, confident of the future. Now, the past held no interest for her, and the future no hope. It stretched before her like a desolate waste that offered neither comfort nor warmth, if it could not also offer her Nat.

'I'll hold the tow until we're further out, and I can see if she'll work under her own power.'

'I suppose I'll work again, but the power will be gone,' Dee acknowledged to herself drearily, and wondered for the first time, with the insight of fellow feeling, if she had chanced upon the secret that lay behind so much of what the world called dedication. For some, the lucky ones, the dedication was genuine, fired by inspiration and nurtured by interest. But for the others, the unlucky ones, could not the long hours of seeming devotion to their self-imposed tasks be nothing more than a defence erected against otherwise empty hours, empty hearts, and the pain of memories that could no longer be endured?

Nat waited for what seemed an endless time while the tug slowly forged ahead, out to sea, towing the smack behind it smoothly and without effort, until the mournful tolling of the bell-buoy grew faint in the distance, and the broken water that marked the length of the mudbank disappeared in the general turbulence of the rising sea.

Whooo! Whooo!

Nat reached up a casual hand and gave the hooter cord two sharp tugs.

'For goodness' sake,' Dee exploded angrily, 'why didn't you warn me you were going to signal?' The unexpected blare made her jump violently, and set her already taut nerves jangling. Her reaction brought a quick grin to Nat's lips, and her temper flared. 'What did you make that infernal noise for, anyway?' she demanded. It was nothing more than small boy mischief, designed to startle her, she decided irately.

'I need to stop the tug for a while,' Nat pointed out reasonably. 'We're well away from the mudbank now, and if the prop's still in one piece,' his tone questioned whether it was, and blamed her if it was not, and her lips tightened ominously, but before she could say anything he resumed, 'if the prop's still in one piece it's better to take the smack into harbour under her own power. She's easier to manoeuvre that way, and it's cheaper on fuel than towing her,' he added practically.

'You'd got it all worked out before you came aboard, hadn't you?' she asked sarcastically, and he sent her a level glance.

'There has to be a system of signals,' he told her with infuriating reasonableness. 'If you'd noticed,' his voice took on a thin edge, 'I didn't bring the loudhailer along with me when I boarded the smack.' He turned away from her towards the control panel, and Dee held her breath.

Would the engine start? And if it did, would the prop turn? Or had it been twisted out of all recognition by submerged wreckage?

The familiar chug of the engine responded to his touch, and he flicked a glance at her over his shoulder as he reached for the gear knob.

'Keep your fingers crossed,' he bade her drily, and slid the lever into forward gear.

Her hands were so tightly clenched she could not have crossed her fingers if she had wanted to. Her nails dug ridges into her clammy palms, and it was only with a supreme effort of self-control that she resisted the urge to clap her hands over her ears to stifle the sound of screaming machinery as tortured propeller blades fought to perform the task that hopelessly twisted metal made them no longer capable of.

The sound did not come. The neutral chugging increased in speed to a steady drone, and the fishing smack lifted its bow to the sea, and forged ahead, released into its own element again.

'There's nothing wrong below,' Nat commented quietly, and Dee leaned back weakly against the bulkhead. Now the tension was over, she felt sick.

'You were lucky.' Nat sent her a probing glance. 'I'm going to cast off the line,' he added, and strode past her to the wheelhouse door, leaving her alone. She watched him go, hating his implied criticism. Hating him, she told herself angrily, loathing the circumstances into which she had been forced, and unable to do anything about them. She let out a long breath that was half a sob, and with a sudden decisive thrust she pushed herself off the bulkhead and hurried to the door.

'I won't accept blame for what's happened,' she repudiated responsibility for simple lack of experience. Accidents could happen to anyone, she told herself fiercely, even to Nat. She shook away a small voice that reminded her Nat was unlikely ever to find himself in such a situation, and with a determined tilt of her chin she followed him across the deck to the rail. He straightened from releasing the towing line, which even as she joined him slid back across the ship's side into the sea, and with a wave of his hand to the figure on the bridge of the tug, Nat turned to go back to the wheelhouse—and found Dee beside him.

'You can go back on to the tug yourself now,' she announced determinedly. He could follow his line across the side, and good riddance! she told herself angrily. She would take the smack back into harbour herself. Stubbornly she refused to thank him for rescuing her. He did not warrant her thanks. He had done it for a price, she reminded herself hardly, and he had exacted that price to the full, and she herself had paid in a coin which she found infinitely more expensive than mere money. Her pride. It smarted still at the memory, and gave an edge to her voice as she added, 'I'll take the smack back into harbour myself.'

'It's normal practice to finish the job you've been paid for.' His look raked her face, bringing the ready colour to her cheeks, and her eyes sparked angrily, but the next instant she knew a traitorous thankfulness when Nat took the wheel and turned the vessel broadside on to the sea, running it parallel with the mudbank, reversing the route of her outward journey. The smack staggered and lurched on the turn, and she grabbed hastily at the wheelhouse door for support.

'The blow's getting up some strength,' Nat remarked laconically as he swung the wheel.

'I can see that,' she retorted tartly. She had been too occupied until now to notice how rough the water had become. As the boat turned sideways on to the waves, they hurled themselves against its sides with frightening force, making the muscles of Nat's arms knot as he held the wheel steady against the power of the water. Dee watched him in silence, keeping her thoughts to herself, but honesty forced her to admit that she could not have held the boat steady herself under such conditions. She lacked the necessary height to exert sufficient pull on the wheel, and her arms did not possess the whipcord strength of Nat's hard-muscled members.

'Hold tight, I'm going to swing her round for a straight run in.' He brought the smack hard round and faced it into the harbour entrance, but even inside, Dee discovered, the water was still rough enough to make her thankful that it was Nat, and not she, who had the task of berthing the vessel. The waves broke in showers of spray against the harbour wall. Safe inside the barrier, she turned to watch the display, and saw that the tug was following them in. Like a sheepdog, driving an errant member of the flock before it back into the fold, she thought, and resentment drowned her thankfulness, so that when they approached the Archer quay she snapped at Nat, critically.

'You're berthing in the wrong place. Our tie-up's further along the quay.'

'It looks as if someone's poached your parking slot,' he grinned, and the grin stung her into fury as a quick glance confirmed that their normal berth was indeed occupied by one of her uncle's other fishing boats. Under any other circumstances it would not have mattered to her, by tradition that area of the quay was occupied by the fishing fleet, and if she had been at the wheel of the smack herself she would simply have berthed somewhere else, and thought no more about it. Now, it annoyed her beyond measure that Nat had noticed the space was occupied and she had not.

With deft hands he swung the smack into its berth, his confident skill making the process look deceptively easy. Dee acknowledged ruefully to herself that in her hands the fenders would have taken a lot more punishment than the gentle bumping Nat gave them, as he brought the vessel to rest against the quayside, and spoke to her casually.

'She'll do for the night here. Now we'll see to your fish.'

'Hugh will attend to those for me,' she told him shortly. It was bad enough to have to suffer the indignity of being brought ashore under a cloud of incompetence, without having Nat take charge of her catch as well.

'Hugh's still on the tug,' he answered her evenly.

'On the tug?' Her forehead creased in bewilderment. 'What's Hugh doing on your tug? He's one of our skippers!' A sudden thought silenced her in mid-speech, but not for long. She burst out angrily, 'I suppose poaching another man's employees while he's in hospital makes it easy for you to crew your own vessel again,' she accused him bitterly.

'Don't be silly.' His scorn was belittling, and she drew in an angry breath.

'It doesn't seem silly to me. Or honourable, either,' she flashed.

'It *is* silly, if you stop to think about it,' he insisted. 'Can you imagine any man who's risen to being skipper of his own vessel being content to crew for someone else?' he asked contemptuously, and she flushed hotly, then went deathly white.

'Then why . . .?' It still did not explain how her uncle's skipper came to be working on the tug.

'Hugh came out with George and me for the sole purpose of rescuing you from the consequences of your own foolhardiness,' he rubbed salt into her already smarting wounds with remorseless vigour.

'So that's how you knew where I'd gone.' She had wondered how he managed to track her down so easily.

'That's how I knew,' he confirmed grimly, 'and it's a good job you mentioned to Hugh where you intended to make for, otherwise none of us would have known in which direction to look. What on earth possessed you to take the smack out in the first place?' he demanded angrily. 'Hugh told you there was a blow on the way. Surely....'

'It's my uncle's boat,' her chin rose proudly, defiantly, 'I've got every right to take it out, whenever I choose.' How dared he question her actions? she asked herself stormily.

'I'm not questioning your rights,' he read her thoughts with uncanny accuracy. 'I'm questioning your sense,' he retorted scathingly, and the look on his face said he really meant her sanity. Dee's fists clenched into tight balls inside her anorak pockets, gripping the nearest thing they found there, trying to hold on to her vanishing self control. Her fingers possessed themselves of something round, and hard, and twisted the ten-pence piece angrily round and round, expending her fury on the innocent silver coin that she had received in change for a chocolate bar, and left forgotten in her pocket afterwards. A small detached part of her mind remembered the chocolate bar distinctly. She had eaten it on a grassy bank in the sunshine, and it seemed a very long time ago since she had enjoyed the sweetness of it, and the peace of her surroundings. Would her heart ever know such peace again? she wondered drearily.

'It takes an amateur to ignore danger.' Nat gave her no quarter. 'You don't seem to think being rescued from the mudbank even warrants a thank-you,' he accused her, in a tone that said he regretted having gone to such trouble on her behalf.

'Why should you expect thanks, when you've already been paid for your services?' she flung back at him bitterly, stung by his accusation. She would never forgive him for exacting that payment, she vowed. Never! 'But if it's thanks you want,' the silver ten-pence piece was hard between her fingers, its milled edge cutting into her flesh with the force of her grip, 'if it's thanks you want, then take this.' Her hand came out of her pocket, her fingers gripping the ten-pence piece, and on an angry impulse she thrust the coin hard into his palm.

'A tip is the usual expression of gratitude, over and above payment for services rendered,' she taunted him bitterly.

CHAPTER SEVEN

She should not have done it.

Sharp fear pierced through her, even as she thrust the coin into his hand. His fingers closed over it with a hard grip, and the impulse died within her before she loosed the silver bit, but it was too late to take it back again, or even to wish she had not given it to him in the first place. It was too late to do anything, except to face Nat's rock-hard glare, his rock-hard face, and watch with widening eyes the tiny pulse at the point of his jawbone throb like a drum beat with the intensity of his anger against her. Her courage quailed before the storm to come, as he spoke through clenched teeth,

'I ought to spank you for that!'

His punishment was far more effective than a spanking could be. He made her pay for every single penny of the regretted ten-penny piece. With a deadly expertise his lips exacted a payment over and above that which he had already taken on account. With cold fury he tossed her frail defences to the winds, and she lay helpless in his arms, unable to withstand the strength of his hold, the fire of his kisses, that parted her lips and took her breath, and when she longed to cry, 'Stop! Stop!' they denied her utterance, and all the sound she could make was a tiny whimper, and Nat silenced that, too, with the implacable force of his lips pressing down upon her own. It seemed a lifetime of agony to Dee before at last his fury waned, and he released her, leaving her spent and breathless, and close to tears, not because he kissed her, but because he no longer did, and her deprived heart cried out at the unendurable agony of its loss as he thrust her away from him, roughly rejecting her, and called out to the figure on the bridge of the tug that was even now nosing towards its place on the quay next to them.

'Throw down a line, and I'll tie up for you!'

He left her standing on the deck. He spun away from her, swung over the rail on to the quayside, and tied the hawsers round the bollards with an expert twist, while Dee stood irresolute, not wanting to be left behind, not wanting to join him.

'I'll box the fish,' she decided. It would delay the need to follow Nat on to the quay. But when she turned to the fish she found she could not touch them. She did not know how to start, she discovered a fresh humiliation, her uncle had always done it for her before, and she turned from her flaccid catch with shuddering aversion.

'I'll see to the fish for you, Miss Lawrence.'

It was Hugh. Blessed, friendly, reliable Hugh, who stood beside her, capably removing this latest problem from her overburdened shoulders, removing herself from the smack, and back on to the grateful stability of the quayside.

'I'll clean them and box them in ice, ready for you to pick up when you collect your car tomorrow morning,' he promised comfortably. 'Steady up the steps, now, they're slippy with the spray,' and he lent her a big, friendly hand to help her walk up the steps, a hand that did not send electric shocks through her fingers when she touched it, so that she could grasp it with confidence, and smile her thanks at him when she reached the quayside, and try to ignore Nat's scowl. It blackened until it nearly resembled the sky as she said to the fishing skipper,

'Goodbye, and thanks, Hugh. I'll see you tomorrow.'

'Where are you going now?' Nat demanded in an ominous voice.

'Home, of course.' Dee halted in her tracks, genuinely surprised. Where did he think she was going? she wondered angrily. It was nothing to do with him where she went, anyway. 'I want my tea.' Suddenly she realised she felt hollow inside.

'Tea?' He stared at her incredulously. 'It's a bit late for tea, or hadn't you realised what time it is?'

'I didn't put my watch on when I came out,' she replied shortly.

'Then I'll enlighten you,' he did so grimly, 'it's nearly eight o'clock.'

'Eight o' . . . I don't believe it!' she gasped. No wonder the light was beginning to fade. She had put the closing dusk down to the rising storm, she had never given the time a thought. She had a moment's qualm about the number of hours she had been away from Cliff House. Her aunt would have returned home long since, and must be wondering where she had gone to.

'By this time your aunt will probably have alerted the coastguard, and reported you missing.' Nat read her thoughts with uncanny accuracy, and caused the qualm to deepen. She had not got as far as thinking about the coastguards. 'It's a good job I brought my car with me,' he added significantly.

'I'll walk home.' The last thing she felt she wanted was another ride in Nat's car just now.

'You'll do no such thing.' He took hold of her arm in a determined grasp and steered her towards the Rover. 'You're coming in the car with me, it'll save your aunt another half-hour of needless worry, and she can call off any search that might have been started for you.'

He hustled her into the passenger seat, and the car was under way before Dee remembered she had not told her aunt she intended to take out the fishing smack in the first place, so there was no question of the coastguards mounting a search for her. She half turned to get out of the car, she even had her hand on the door handle, but Nat accelerated off the hard and on to the road with a speed that made it impossible for her to do anything but sit back again in her seat, and fume in silence.

'But of course I wasn't worried.' Her aunt looked mildly surprised at Dee's hasty apology when they went indoors, and she instantly regretted offering it while Nat was present. It was tantamount to an admission that his silent accusation of lack of consideration was justified.

'I needn't have given him that satisfaction,' she berated her own over-active conscience, while her aunt continued happily,

'You said in the note you left for me that you might be late in for tea.' Dee flashed Nat a barbed glance, which said she wasn't quite without consideration, since she had left a note, but with infuriating timing he managed to look in the other direction while Martha Lawrence finished placidly, 'So when you didn't come back in time for tea, Helen and I had ours. I said you'd probably met Nat and gone off together somewhere nice.'

That was hardly the description she would have applied to their outing, Dee told herself drily, and wondered uneasily what her relative would have to say when she knew that their outing had ended in the fishing smack being towed off the mudbank by the tug, at dire risk to the smack, her own life, and her uncle's insurance policy.

'How he'll enjoy telling her,' she thought angrily, and waited in vain for Nat to launch into an account of the incident, to her own discredit. To her surprise he remained silent on the subject, and asked instead,

'How did you find Mr Lawrence this afternoon?'

Dee felt unaccountably let down by his restraint. If he had taunted her with the doings of the afternoon, she could have hit back. She felt very much like hitting back. But his silence denied her the opportunity. It was almost, she thought irately, as if he considered the whole affair to be too trivial to mention.

'Oh, Frank's champing at the bit,' her aunt smiled,

'but there's only a few days to go now until he comes home, and at least this year he's got the perfect excuse not to attend the annual ball at the Town Hall.' She turned to Dee appealingly. 'Your uncle wondered if you'd go in his place. He thinks the family ought to be represented, and I can't possibly sit out an entire evening there myself.' Her aunt was not above using her arthritis as a perfect excuse either, Dee thought ruefully, noting the twinkle in her elderly relative's eyes.

'I can't go on my own,' Dee protested. It would be bad enough to cope with the evening under any circumstances, her memory of the last time she had attended was hardly inspiring, and the prospect of facing it alone was too much. She shook her head firmly.

'Perhaps Nat could go with you?' her aunt suggested guilelessly. 'The invitation's for two people.'

'No!'

Dee went scarlet with mortification. She did not know where to look. She did not dare to look at Nat. How could her aunt be so tactless? She writhed with impotent embarrassment. 'Nat will be going with his father and brothers.' She released him immediately from the embarrassment of having to refuse to take her. The only thing more awful than her aunt shanghaiing an unwilling escort for her, would be for Nat to refuse point blank to take her. She felt every nerve in her body prickle at the prospect of such humiliation.

'My family will be there in sufficient strength, without needing my presence,' Nat said smoothly.

'They won't notice the absence of the Lawrence clan either, not just for this one year,' Dee interrupted him breathlessly. 'Everyone knows Uncle Frank's in hospital after his accident, so no one will expect him. I'll tell him I can't go, when I see him tomorrow. I've got to go in to take the fish I caught. . . .' She stopped. She meant to tell her aunt about the fishing trip, after Nat had gone home.

The last thing she wanted was his presence at her confessional.

'You bought your uncle some fish?' Her aunt looked doubtful. 'Was that wise? Fish from the shops will probably taste just as stale to him as the fish fingers.'

'No, I caught some for him this afternoon,' Dee answered reluctantly. 'I took the smack out to the other side of the mudbank, and. . . .' Her words choked her.

'And brought home some prime plaice. Hugh's putting them on ice until tomorrow,' Nat finished for her smoothly, and Dee stared at him with disbelief.

Why didn't he tell her aunt he had rescued the smack from off the mudbank, and get it over with? she asked herself, tension tautening her nerves almost to breaking point. It was almost as if he was storing up the incident, holding it over her head with a cat-and-mouse kind of cruelty, waiting for the right opportunity to turn an item of news into a bombshell.

'You'll have to take the fish into the hospital first thing in the morning,' her aunt cautioned, 'or it won't be any use to them for Friday lunch. I'll give your uncle a ring this evening, and he can warn them it's coming,' she decided.

'At the same time, you can tell him his ticket for the ball won't be wasted,' Nat put in smoothly, and Dee gasped at his effrontery.

'I've just said I won't go,' she flared angrily.

'It's a pity not to use the invitation, so I'll take you up on your offer.' Nat accepted as if Dee had not spoken, and she gritted her teeth and forced back the angry words that rose to her lips as Martha Lawrence said with obvious pleasure,

'That's settled, then. Frank wouldn't like the family not to be represented at all.'

'Nat's hardly "family",' Dee pointed out shortly when they were alone at supper later. 'I can't imagine what

Uncle Frank will say, when he knows one of the Archer family is going in his place.' Her forehead creased in a frown.

'He already knows,' her aunt replied, and Dee stared at her, astounded.

'But . . . an Archer?' Words failed her.

'Frank's got nothing against Nat,' her aunt pointed out reasonably, and added, 'he's got nothing against Wordesley Archer any more. Oh, I know they bristle like a pair of hedgehogs when they meet one another, but it's simply habit, it can't be dislike any more. Their rivalry was all so long ago,' she smiled reminiscently. 'At their age, it's high time they put all those things behind them and behaved sensibly,' she finished, briskly practical.

'I'll have to get a new dress.' Between her aunt and Nat, Dee felt driven into a corner. She longed to lash out, to free herself from the sheer pressure of events, but she could hardly lash out at an elderly relative, and Nat had gone home an hour ago and was safely out of reach, she thought humourlessly. Even the prospect of a new dress was for once no balm to her ruffled feelings, and her frustration was not eased when she reached the quayside the next morning on her way to collect her car. The wind had backed off during the night, sparing the town the worst of the threatened storm, and the fishing skipper called to her cheerfully from the deck of his smack as she passed.

'I've put the box of fish in the back of Mr Archer's van for you, Miss Lawrence.'

'Whatever for?' Dee asked him, frowning. 'I shall want the box in the boot of my own car.'

'Dunno, miss, but Mr Archer said to do it,' Hugh disclaimed responsibility. 'He'll have his reasons, no doubt,' he said comfortably.

'They'd better be good ones,' Dee gritted through set teeth, and turned to confront Nat as he descended with a catlike surety of tread down the plank from the tug berthed nearby.

'How dare you appropriate my box of fish?' she blazed as soon as he was within earshot. Last night, as she surrendered to sleep, she had determined that the next time she met him she would remain cool, distant, and above all things, calm. And now, the moment they met, it was like putting a match to tinder. All her good resolutions fled to the wind, and she turned on him furiously. 'You've no right to give instructions to Hugh. He's not your employee.' That, on top of confiscating her fish, proved too much, and her temper snapped.

'He's not your employee either.' Their glances met, clashed, twin steels in a fencing match that seemed to renew itself each time they met, but which this time she was determined not to lose.

'I want the box of fish put in the boot of *my* car,' she demanded, goaded beyond endurance by his manner. 'I caught it, and I intend to take it to the hospital myself.'

'You won't be able to,' he told her calmly, 'at least, not in your own car.'

'My car's ready, I'm on my way to collect it now.'

'Your car isn't ready,' he contradicted her coolly, 'I checked when I went to fill up the van first thing this morning. The foreman told me a water hose had gone, and they won't have a replacement piece of the correct size until late this afternoon.'

'In that case, I'll leave the fish until tomorrow, so you can take it out of your van and give it back to Hugh,' she snapped, unable to gainsay his argument, and further irked by the fact that if she did not go into town today she would not be able to obtain a dress for the ball. She had not bothered to bring a long dress with her when she came to Penzyn, she had not considered it would be necessary. Now, she would have preferred the extra time to look round and buy something she liked. Choosing in haste usually ended disastrously, and since she was committed to going to the ball with Nat as her escort, she intended her dress to do justice to the occasion, if only to give her the confidence she sorely needed when she was in his company.

'Your uncle will have told the hospital to expect the fish today,' he commented, and made no move to open his van doors and remove the offending box of plaice. 'Your aunt said last night she'd phone to say it was coming.'

Her aunt had phoned. Dee spoke to her uncle as well, and his unfeigned delight at the prospect of fresh fish for lunch instead of the hated fish fingers put her in a dilemma. She had promised she would bring it in, and now she was left with the choice of breaking her promise, or allowing Nat, once more, to have his own way.

'I've got to go into town to see Wainwrights, the brokers,' the latter commented casually. 'If you don't want to come in yourself, I can drop the fish at the hospital for you....'

'I'll come,' she decided instantly. He should not deliver her fish, she told herself stubbornly. It was her catch, and it was her privilege to take it in. She looked up and caught the sudden flare of laughter deep in his black eyes. Laughter at her expense. A hot tide of angry colour flooded her cheeks, and she bit her lip, on the point of changing her mind no matter what the consequences, when Hugh broke in considerately.

'Let me hold your coat and bag while you get in the van, Miss Lawrence.' The fishing skipper reached out and took her accoutrements with an olde-worlde courtesy that at any other time Dee would have found refreshing, and been suitably grateful for, and now discovered that it enmeshed her, so that she had no choice but to get into the van or make a scene, and she wanted to do neither. She paused, then with a hopeless shrug she turned to the van as Nat held open the door for her, and got in silently, and hated the merriment in his eyes. Hated Nat, she told herself fiercely, and took her bag and coat from Hugh and busied herself with straightening them so that she need not look up as the door slammed on her with a decisive bang that said Nat had intended her to come with him all along, and she had time to wonder, when it was too late to do anything about it, why she had not thought to check with the garage herself, to make sure that his story was not a mere fabrication, designed to once more oblige her to do as he wished.

'I'll carry the fish into the hospital myself.' She got out of the van at the hospital entrance, and faced him squarely

'Go ahead.'

His prompt acquiesence should have warned her. A small doubt impinged on her mind even as he reached out and opened the rear double doors of the van, and her eyes widened as the doubt blossomed into acute dismay, and the reason for Nat's apparently meek obedience of her demand confronted her.

'I can't possibly lift that!'

She had forgotten the fish would be packed in ice. That which Hugh put on them the night before would have melted long since, but he must have put fresh ice in the box before placing it in Nat's van that morning. It glistened coldly, winking at her with solemn mockery, diamond-bright, and crystal-hard, and indisputably heavy. Far too heavy for Dee to lift unaided.

'I can't possibly lift that!' she gasped.

'There doesn't seem to be any other way to get it out of the van,' Nat commented, and Dee could have hit him for the amusement in his voice, although his face remained grave. 'Unless, of course,' he paused and looked at her levelly, and the laughter was gone from his eyes, and in its place was a challenge, and something else she could not define, something that unaccountably confused her, and caused her to drop her eyes away from his, unable to meet his look as he continued smoothly, 'Unless, of course, you were to ask me nicely, to lift it for you?'

'What do you mean, ask you nicely?' she snapped. The last thing she felt like at the moment, was being nice to Nat.

'W-e-e-ll——' he quirked a considering eyebrow, and her patience gave way.

'Consider yourself asked,' she capitulated ungraciously, and hoped uncharitably, as he picked up the weighty box with enviable ease, that some of the ice might fall off under his feet. Just sufficient, she thought hopefully, to make him slip and measure his length on the pavement. She did not wish him physical harm, and since they were at the hospital entrance anyway the Casualty Department would take care of any bumps, she thought callously. She merely wanted to dent his chauvinistic, egotistical male arrogance.... She ran out of suitable adjectives as well as hope when he lifted the box easily, and strode surefooted through the hospital entrance as if it was no more weighty than a feather pillow. He reappeared a few minutes later with not even a sign of dampness on his jacket to show what he had been carrying, and Dee scowled ungratefully as he said,

'They were very pleased with your gift. Now you can go and look for your dress with a clear conscience. Blue would suit you. It's always a good idea to match your eyes.'

'I'll get pink, green, yellow. Any other colour except blue,' she decided mutinously. 'And I'll go back home by train when I've finished shopping,' she added out loud for Nat's benefit. 'I'll be simply ages getting what I want,' she defied him to demand that she present herself back at the van at a certain time. 'I'll go home when it suits me,' she decided independently, and faced him with her chin held high.

'That's a lady's privilege,' was all he answered, and her defiance collapsed like a pricked balloon. If he had argued, tried to insist that she accepted a lift home in the van afterwards, he would give her the perfect excuse to let her pent-up anger spill over. In her present mood she would welcome a showdown with Nat. Instead he remarked appreciatively.

'It's useful having the hospital so close to the middle of the town, the shopping centre's handy without having to walk too far. Wainwrights is the other way.' He did not sound at all regretful that they would not walk together even the short distance to the shopping centre. 'I'll leave the van in this park and cut across the cathedral grounds to their offices. I hope you manage to find what you're looking for,' he added politely, and with a nod and a smile—if he had been wearing a hat she felt sure he would have doffed it, she thought sarcastically—he left her and strode across the greensward flanking the cathedral. She watched him until he disappeared from sight beyond a clump of trees, and found her feet curiously reluctant to take her in the opposite direction towards the main shopping street.

'I don't know what I'm looking for,' she confessed to herself mournfully. Except Nat, her heart reminded her. But she had found Nat. It was he who had not found her, and never would. The thought took away the colour from the day, the adventure from the shopping expedition, even her interest in the dresses that were variously pretty, stylish, and would have suited her if she could be bothered to try them on, but to her lacklustre eyes each looked as uninspiring as the one before, so that by mid morning her spirits were reduced to zero, and her feet felt weary with trecking from store to store on a seemingly hopeless quest to find something that would fit the occasion.

Or something that would please Nat? She thrust the unwelcome thought from her sharply, but she could not thrust away the fact that out of the bevy of dresses which she had looked at so far, only the blue ones came near to pleasing her.

'I'll have one more try, and if I'm not successful then I'll go home.' Refreshed, and with her determination strengthened by a cup of coffee, she made her way to the only other shop that was left. It was small, exclusive, and when she wanted something really special she had purchased there before. This occasion was one for a really special dress, and it was because she was to represent her family, and not because Nat was to be her escort, she told herself firmly.

It was blue. It was almost inevitable, she told herself resignedly. The other dresses in her size, yellow, and green, and a delicate lilac, were all gorgeous, but,

'The blue is quite perfect.'

For once, the assistant was not merely using sales talk. The dress fitted Dee like a glove. The softly draped neckline fanned into long shoulders, and covered the tops of her arms without need of a sleeve, ideal for a summer ball. It framed the delicate bone structure of her face; accentuated the colour of her eyes, and fell in a swirl of midnight blue to just the right length from the floor. It shimmered slightly as she moved, the rich colour cunningly interwoven with a silver thread that caught the light as she turned. It reminded her of the warm blue mystery of tropical nights, beribboned with the silver of a tropical moon. Nights such as Nat must have seen many times, and, anguish twisted her heart at the thought, would see again when the *Sea Wind* bore him away from Penzyn, and out of her life for ever.

'It really *does* something for you,' the assistant said admiringly.

But not enough, if it could not give her Nat. . . .

'I'll take it,' she decided on the spur of the moment. She had no option, really, she defended her impulse. She had been to all the other shops in the town once already, and rejected everything they had to offer. She was taking this dress because there was nothing else left, not because Nat wanted her to wear something blue. . . .

'Why don't you walk out into the shop and look at

yourself in the long mirrors there?' the assistant suggested. 'There's more room there than in the cubicle.'

Dee did not want to have a closer look at the dress. She did not want to even think about it, any more than she wanted to think about Nat, and tropical moons. She just wished the assistant would wrap it up so that she could flee the shop and hide herself at Cliff House, and not think about anything, or anybody, she wished fiercely, until the ball was over. But in the face of the girl's friendly persuasion it seemed churlish not to respond, so she stepped outside the cubicle reluctantly to face her own reflection in the mirror-lined walls of the shop.

The material clung softly to the gently rounded curves of her slender figure, deepening the blue of her eyes, and what they saw in the mirror brought a sudden sparkle to them that matched the silver thread in the dress. Even in broad daylight the delicate, floating material gave her dainty figure an almost ethereal look that made her first glance and then stare at herself with wide-eyed disbelief, then the sparkle deepened, and a tiny smile curved the corners of her lips, and her confidence reasserted itself in a reassuring flood. Then she raised her eyes still further, attracted by the slight movement from behind her which she took to be the hovering assistant, and discovered instead,

'You!'

Her eyes locked with Nat's through the mirror, hers blue, startled, confused, the sparkle of confidence drowned by dawning anger. How dare he follow her into the dress shop? His were black, laughing, supremely confident, and with a glint in them that suddenly made it difficult for Dee to meet his look.

'I saw you come in, so I thought I'd come along and make sure I approved your choice,' he grinned.

'It's immaterial to me whether you approve or not,' she flashed back crushingly, and wished she had chosen the lilac dress instead. She even opened her mouth to call the assistant and ask her to make the exchange, and found the girl was already coming back with the bill made out, neatly foiling her would-be volte-face. She saw Nat glance at the bill, and took it herself, quickly, determined that he should not see. She still owed him for the chocolates and the cotton wool. She did not owe him for rescuing her from the mudbank; she had paid him in full for that. Abruptly, she turned her back on him and slipped hurriedly back into the blessed privacy of the cubicle, drawing the curtains to with a swish that rattled the hooks on their runners, to shut herself off from his sight.

'Let me help you. These very fine zips are difficult to manage.' It was not the fault of the zip. Her hands trembled so much that her fingers would not hold the tiny latch, and she submitted to the assistant's ministrations, fighting to regain some measure of self-control. The girl whisked the dress over her head and took it away, and Dee donned her own clothes slowly, willing herself to stop shaking, and when she emerged into the shop and faced Nat again, although she still trembled inside her, outwardly at least her poise was restored more or less to normal. She handed the assistant her cheque, and the girl receipted the bill and indicated Nat with a smile. An approving one, Dee noticed.

'She's as gullible as Aunt Martha and Helen,' she thought disgustedly.

'The gentleman offered to carry the box for you,' the girl told her.

'I'd prefer to carry it myself.' She shrugged into her jacket, and held out her hand imperiously for the box. 'I told you not to wait for me. I said I'd go back by train,' she said coldly.

'I know you did, and I didn't,' he answered her back to front, and her anger rose as he retained his hold on the dress box. Unexpectedly, Nat reached out instead and took her outstretched hand in his own. His move took her by surprise, not giving her time to draw back. Once his hand touched her own, she found she could not if she wanted to.

It was like accidentally touching a live electric wire. Her lips parted in silent exclamation, and her eyes widened at the burning shock of it. She wanted to pull her hand away, to run, as fast and as far away from Nat as she could. But her hand seemed to be imbued with a life of its own. Her muscles refused to respond to her will, and her fingers clung to Nat's as if to a lifeline, and she could not loose him if she tried. From what seemed a long distance away, she heard him speak, and quivered as the deep, familiar tones fell on her ears, as an instrument quivers into life at the touch of a musician's fingers on the strings.

'My appointment with Wainwrights took longer than I expected it to,' he said casually. 'I was on the way back to collect the van when I spotted you coming into the shop, so I popped into a little pub I know along the road and booked lunch for us both there. Then I followed you in here,' he informed her coolly. 'I guessed you'd be an age trying on things. Women always are.'

She had not been an age. A flicker of latent rebellion rose within her. She had only tried on the one dress—the blue one. And anyway, how did Nat know how long women took to try on things? Her quick, unguarded glance betrayed what she was thinking, and his ready grin brought the colour to her cheeks without giving her the satisfaction of an answer.

'The pub specialises in barbecued chicken toasted to a turn, with young green peas, and tiny new potatoes, and their lemon meringue pies are out of this world,' he told her gravely.

She tried to blame it on to the fact that she was hungry. One cup of coffee was insufficient to sustain a hard morning shopping, and weariness and hunger *could* have added the final impetus to the irresistible magnetism of Nat's touch on her hand, the overpowering closeness of him beside her, that seemed to fill the shop, her mind, her whole being, so that she could not see anything else, or think about anybody else. With a sigh, she acknowledged herself defeated. She had battled, but she could not battle any longer. Her defences were in ruins, and her armoury was empty. It was a completely successful coup and, she thought half hysterically, Nat did not even know he had won!

'I hope you're hungry?' he enquired.

One tiny part of her still longed to pull her hand away from his; to shout at him that she did not want his food, his company, his lift home; that she was tired of his high-handed attitude, and she would not allow him to order her day for her. But the flicker of rebellion was not strong enough to withstand the stronger yearning of her heart. It died unmourned, and through a mist she heard her own unruly tongue reply,

'I'm starving!'

She could not fight him any more. The mere touch of his fingers on her own did things to her heart that brought a glow to her eyes, a lightness to her head that nothing had ever done before. Reason might blame it on hunger, on tiredness, even on the silver-blue witchery of her dress, but the sweet dawning womanhood inside her knew that it was none of these things, but something intangible, and yet stronger than life itself, that held her in a grip which made that of the mudbank seem weak by comparison, an all-embracing power that stormed her defences, crumbled her resistance, and left her breathless and defeated.

And her heart triumphant.

The assistant spoke to her, saying goodbye, and somehow Dee replied in what to her surprise sounded like a more or less normal voice, as she allowed Nat to steer her to the door without protest. She clung to his hand, needing his guidance because she felt lightheaded, and too bemused to notice in which direction he took her. She was only conscious of Nat holding her, Nat beside her, and any hunger she felt was for the feel of Nat's arms around her, the touch of his lips on her own. Her tiredness was only in her mind, that surrendered at last to the victorious persistence of her heart, which insisted that Nat could do with her what he willed, lead her wherever he would, and she would follow.

He sat her at a corner table at the inn, in a small, cosy inglenook with dark old beams overhead, and at any other time she would have gloried in her surroundings, but now they passed unnoticed, because she had eyes only for Nat. The waiter brought her barbecued chicken and young green peas and tiny new potatoes, but the food she ate was ambrosia. He offered tiny cups of aromatic coffee, but the liquid she drank was nectar. And when finally they emerged, and returned to the car park replete and rested, she rode not in a van, but on a rosy cloud, so that when Nat drew to a halt on the forecourt of the garage in Penzyn she stared about her uncomprehendingly. He should not have stopped. She wanted the ride to go on for ever.

'Why . . . ?'

'Your car should be ready by now. They promised it for late afternoon.'

She nearly said, 'What car?' and stopped herself just in time.

'You were so absorbed in trying on dresses, you forgot all about your car,' he accused her teasingly, and if she could have spoken she could not have denied the truth of what he said. But the lump in her throat stopped her from speaking, and when she swallowed and got her voice back, the moment had gone, and there was nothing left for her to do except walk with dragging feet across the garage forecourt, and somehow blink back the tears that made her car and the garage foreman's cheerful face waver in front of her eyes, because driving her own car meant she must part company with Nat before she felt the journey had hardly begun. And then she must go the rest of the way on her own. It seemed somehow symbolic, and the food of the gods turned into a leaden weight in her stomach, and the rosy cloud lost its bright glow, and darkened as if with impending storm.

She heard herself thank the foreman, thank Nat politely for the meal and the lift. She even smiled and waved a hand in what she hoped would deceive them both into thinking was a cheerful leave taking, as she turned away from the garage towards the road to Cliff House, and the bright little Mini that had been her pride and joy now seemed empty, and cold. As empty and cold as her heart. . . .

Skip stood at the gate when she drew up, and she retained enough presence of mind to make her dab a hasty foot on the brake when she caught sight of the dog, but the little terrier had learned his lesson well, and remained meekly, and quietly, behind the fence, reserving his welcome until she was through the gate and on to the path, and reaching for the chocolate drop that she knew she should not give him, and had not the heart to refuse.

'Your dress is a dream.'

To her relief her aunt did not seem to notice her quietness, and if she did she probably put it down to weariness after a day shopping. Dee gave her a brief account of her doings, then curled up in an armchair with a magazine she found lying on the seat. Reading would give her a perfect excuse for not talking. Suddenly, she did not want to share even the memory of the bright bubble in which she had floated, if only for a while. It was too fragile, too precious, to be touched by any hands other than her own—or Nat's.

'There's an article about Nat in that magazine you're reading.' Her aunt knitted placidly, unaware of how her niece's heart lurched just at the sound of his name. 'Helen left it. She thought it might interest you.'

The magazine was typical of Helen, Dee thought with a

slight smile—glossy, and dreadfully expensive. Perhaps Nat was a contributor? She leafed through the pages, her curiosity aroused. Her aunt had said, 'an article *about* Nat,' so he could not have written it himself.

His photograph stared at her from the top of the page. She forced her eyes to look at it, to glance at the title underneath, and—her palpitating heart felt as if it was going to stop, and never beat again—read over again the lead-in underneath.

'Nat Archer, the celebrated writer and photographer ... an exclusive series of articles and pictures specially commissioned for this magazine ...' and, in words that seemed to leap out at her from the page, striking her with the force of a physical blow, '... a two-year journey, starting shortly, in which Nat Archer will bring the world and its people to your doorstep, in picture and story.'

'Are you feeling all right, Dee?' Through a daze she became aware that her aunt was surveying her concernedly, and she got to her feet, and discovered that her legs trembled, threatening not to hold her.

'I'm a bit tired, that's all.' She felt the blood drain from her face. She felt grey and lifeless all over, as well as sick. 'I think I'll have an early night. I'll take the magazine with me, and have a read before I go to sleep.' She successfully sidetracked her aunt, and managed not to stumble until she closed the drawing room door behind her, and reached the bottom of the stairs. There, she clung to the newel post with hands that felt clammy and weak, as weak as her knees that all but refused the task of climbing the stairs, and collapsed when she finally reached the blessed haven of her own room, where she could fling herself and the magazine face downwards on the bed, and let the tears flow, and sob aloud the question,

'Why, Nat? Why?'

And sob again, because there was no answer. Only the inescapable, printed fact that Nat would shortly start on a two-year journey round the world, commissioned by the magazine. A journey that would leave her behind, the preparations for which must be occupying his thoughts and his time to the exclusion of almost everything else, but although she had been with him for most of the day, chatting over a long lunch, and driving with him in the privacy of the van, he had not said a word to her about his plans.

'Why, Nat? Why?' her agonised heart cried into the pillow, and found only one cruel answer.

Nat had not talked to her about his future plans because she was not important enough to him to discuss them with. Because he did not consider she had any part in them.

CHAPTER EIGHT

'SOMETHING borrowed, something blue.'

'It's a dance dress, not a wedding dress!'

Dee's tone was sharp, and she instantly regretted it. She was grateful for the loan of the silver stole, and the silver slippers. Helen glanced up from where she stooped to fasten the buckle of one of the slippers, and her eyes registered surprise at the sharpness, and Dee forced a conciliatory smile.

'It's very good of you to lend them to me.'

She *was* grateful, she told herself remorsefully. She would have been more grateful still if Helen had kept her tactless quotation to herself. But Helen was not to know that it was tactless.... She sighed, sharply, and turned with relief when her uncle spoke, safely returned since that very morning to his own armchair by the window.

'You make me wish I was going to the ball after all.' The elderly fisherman regarded her with frank pride. 'You look lovely, my dear.'

'I wish you were coming,' Dee answered with complete honesty. She would have been safe with Uncle Frank. Safe from the pain and the heartache, and the desperate, trembling uncertainty of waiting for Nat to come and pick her up and take her to the ball.

'Like Cinderella,' she thought, and her heart twisted. Her own 'stroke of midnight' would sound all too soon, only it would not be she who would disappear, but Nat, on his two years long journey round the world, to new places, new people, new things to capture his attention, and allow him easily to forget the brief summer sojourn in Penzyn. Would he, she wondered unhappily, bring out his photographs to amuse his guests at Christmas time, perhaps somewhere in the warm blue mystery of a tropical night? And, if her picture happened to be among them, the one in the poppy red skirt and the white cotton petticoat with red ribbons flying, if her picture happened to be among them, and some guest asked with idle interest who she might be, would he glance at it, indifferently, perhaps wrinkle his forehead for a moment in thought, then answer,

'I remember taking it, when I was home for a few weeks last summer. But for the life of me I can't remember her name.'

Would he?

Her eyes blurred at the answer, that almost had to be, 'Yes.'

'That's fastened securely enough now, it won't come undone. The strap's still a bit stiff to get through the buckle, that's all.' Helen rose to her feet, and Dee hastily blinked her eyes into clear focus again, as two discreet hoots on the horn of the Rover told her Nat had arrived, and expected her to be ready.

'Well, I must say Nat Archer's got an eye for a lovely girl.' Helen gave Dee an appraising, professional glance, then a warm, affectionate smile.

'He takes after his father for that,' Frank Lawrence growled, and Dee glanced across at him. Had Martha underestimated his dislike of Wordesley Archer and his family? But even as she looked the lined face creased into a youthful grin, and her uncle reached out over his chair arm and clasped Martha's hand in his own. 'The Archer men's eyes are sure enough,' he acknowledged gruffly, 'it's their aim that's not so good.' His own eyes softened in a way that brought a glow to his wife's face, and he finished with satisfaction, 'Their arrows don't always find the target they're intended for.'

'That's how marriage should be. That's how I want mine to be, if I ever get married,' Dee thought wistfully, and raised her eyes to Nat's face as Helen let him in through the door, wondering if she could ever hope to achieve such happiness herself, unless it be with Nat.

'I'm glad Helen's slippers have got high heels.' The thought flashed through her mind, but even the confidence donated by high heels could not stem the wave of shyness that flooded over her as she turned to face Nat's tall, dark figure coming through the door. He had to duck to get under the lintel, and as he straightened up she caught her breath. He looked almost unbelievably handsome.

'Why is it?' she wondered confusedly, 'why is it that evening dress suits dark-haired men so much better than fair-haired ones?' The magpie black and white moulded his lithe, athletic figure in a manner that spoke of the skill of a West End tailor, and he wore it with the ease of custom. He was probably used to formal balls, she thought. And more sophisticated company? Her spirits dropped to zero as her mind added remorselessly, 'Perhaps he regards this evening as a mere provincial get-together. A boring duty dance.' And herself a duty partner, perhaps equally boring? He had been pressed into service as her escort in a manner which made it almost impossible for him to refuse. The memory of it rankled still, galling, humiliating. It belittled herself, and her dress, and her momentary confidence, gained from her high heels, evaporated as she looked up into his face.

His eyes seemed to bore down at her, black, compelling, but the dusk of the late summer evening shadowed the room, masking their expression, making his face inscrutable. Dee could not read in either what he thought of her, or of her dress. She did not want to know, she told herself breathlessly, and flinched as his hand moved towards her, dreading his touch and at the same time longing for it. But when she tore her eyes from his face and looked at his hand, she saw that it held a box, narrow, Cellophane-wrapped, and containing the pale beauty of a flower.

'A lovely dress deserves a corsage,' Nat remarked, and gave it into her nerveless fingers.

'A lovely dress.' He did not say, 'a lovely girl.'

Dee stared numbly down at the flower. It was a silver white carnation, a powder-puff of delicate loveliness, its frilly petals shading to palest pink right at the edge. It reminded her of a ballerina's skirt. She half expected it to rise up and begin to dance. It *did* dance! It blurred and started to waver to and fro in front of her eyes. She gave a gasp, and raised them back to Nat's face, and discovered that was wavering, too.

'Let me fix it on for you.'

He took the box back from her fingers and laid it on the table, opened it, and removed the carnation. As he took the lid off, the sweet, heady perfume of the flower caught at her nostrils. It acted as a restorative, and the room stopped swimming round her, and she drew in a deep breath, savouring the sweetness of it. For ever afterwards she would remember Nat when she breathed the scent of carnations, she told herself, and there was a catch in her voice as she said out loud,

'It's beautiful!'

Then her voice wavered into silence as his fingers touched against her shoulder, skilfully fixing the flower in just the right place to enhance it, and the dress. With the skill of practice? The thought crossed her mind like an ice-cold spear, freezing her words in her throat, killing her joy in his gift. Perhaps Nat always gave a flower to his partner for the evening, regarding it as no more than a normal, routine courtesy?

The white carnation, laced with fronds of double white gypsophila, was perfect for her dress. But it would be perfect with almost any coloured dress. Perhaps, when Nat attended more sophisticated gatherings, with a partner he chose for himself, he bought orchids?

She shivered as she got into the car, and drew the borrowed stole more closely round her shoulders, grateful for the comforting warmth of the mohair. Nat glanced at her as he bent to tuck her dress round her before shutting the door and striding round the car to his own seat. He did not speak, or ask her if she felt cold, but he reached out long fingers and flicked the car heater system into action, and the softly purring engine poured out gentle warmth around her. She lay back in her seat, willing herself to relax, conscious that tonight Nat would dance with her, hold her in his arms probably for the last time, and although her fainting courage urged her to flee and spare herself the pain, another stronger part of her urged her to savour the moments while she could, because soon Nat would be gone, and her life would be empty.

Soon, she too would be gone. Now her uncle was home again there was no reason for her to stay on, but, she thought wistfully, a part of her would always remain in Penzyn, a small ghostly shade in red-ribboned petticoats, dancing barefoot on a shell sand beach. . . .

'Shall we dance?' The floor of the Town Hall was smoother than the beach, perfect for waltzing. But her feet had not stumbled on the beach, so why should they stumble now, clumsy on a perfect floor?

'New shoes?' Nat asked shrewdly.

'Helen lent them to me. They're comfortable, but they've got high heels. I've been wearing flat sandals mostly since I came to Penzyn.'

'You're babbling,' she told herself, and stopped. Nat had that effect on her. She either wanted to shout defiance at him, or she became incoherent. Why, on this their special night together, that might easily be their last, could she not acquit herself with some semblance of poise? she asked herself wretchedly, and tried to gather round herself an armour of self-respect that would hide the ache in her heart, and the icy numbness that crept over her mind every time she thought of Nat going away.

'Take them off and dance in your bare feet,' he murmured, low-voiced, and his eyes glinted with laughter. 'You can dance barefoot—I saw you once before.'

He had seen her on the shell beach, and taken her photograph. Dee looked up at him, protest and responsive laughter struggling for mastery in her mobile face, then she looked down again quickly, and her heart hammered, catching her breath so that she was unable to reply, though even without breath she managed somehow to dance on, willing her feet to continue moving because if they stopped it meant Nat would drop his arms from around her, and that she could not bear. People watching them would probably think they were smiling together at some intimate joke, something special that only they could share. How wrong they would be, she thought bitterly. What would be their reaction if she told them they were talking about a pair of borrowed shoes? she wondered with desperate levity, and did not know whether to giggle or to weep at the reality, as opposed to the dream.

'I can't dance in bare feet, not here.' She found her voice at last, a faint whispered travesty of her normal cheerful tones, but it would have to serve because she did not feel capable of more. In the warm blue mystery of a tropical night, she could dance barefoot under a tropical moon. She could dance barefoot on nails, if necessary, so long as Nat was her partner.

'Then I'll have to hold you up, if you trip over.' He sounded resigned. Bored? But his arm tightened about her, reinforcing his promise, and to anyone looking on it would seem as if he held her close because that was the way it was, with courting couples.

The cruel contradiction closed her eyes with pain, and she discovered that with them closed, she could pretend, with the world shut out, that that was how it really was between herself and Nat. Gratefully she gave herself up to the pretence, because the reality hurt too much. She laid her cheek against his lapel, and her feet followed his skilful guidance, moving to the lilt of Strauss with the easy unison of partners who were born to dance together. The irony of it tore at her heart, but she kept her eyes firmly closed, willing her dream to continue if only for a little while, willing her feet to move, not across a prosaic dance floor, but along a magic silver path made of tropical moonlight.

Strauss fled before the brassy syncopation of modern beat. The orchestra switched to a quickstep, and noise and laughter surged across the ballroom, pricking her bubble, and she opened her eyes to reality as Hugh's voice said from beside her,

'Glad you could come, Miss Lawrence. The ball wouldn't seem the same without someone here from Cliff House.'

She turned, and heard herself being polite to the fishing skipper, greeting his wife, while all the time her heart broke because the quickstep ended and they ceased to dance, and although Nat stood beside her he no longer held her, and in a crowded room she stood on an island of desolation, alone.

'You had a nasty experience, getting stuck on the Whale.' Hugh's wife was cheerfully sympathetic. 'Wasn't it lucky Mr Archer happened to be here with his tug?' The older woman beamed her approval on Nat, and Dee no longer thought it gullible, she felt the same herself now.

'The storm didn't come to anything, luckily,' she answered.

'It hasn't finished with us yet,' Hugh remarked sagely, with the wisdom of a lifetime on the coast. 'The wind backed off, but it's only paused to get its breath. According to the shipping forecast this evening, it's heading back this way.' He grimaced towards Nat and added significantly, 'It's a swinging wind, too, so I'm hoping it'll blow itself out before it reaches us.'

'A swinging wind?' Dee raised puzzled eyes to Nat as they followed the older couple in the direction of the buffet table.

'He means an oscillating wind, swinging between two compass points.'

That about described her own relationship with Nat, she thought ruefully. Her feelings towards him swung between loathing and love, and she swung with them, helplessly, unable to control either her own feelings or her own destiny. Only knowing that unless that destiny included Nat, it left her future bleak and empty, and so far as she was concerned, unwanted. But at least he treated her like an intelligent adult when it came to imparting information, he did not talk down to her, she thought thankfully, as he went on with a grave face,

'If it reaches gale force, that kind of wind creates its own particular kind of havoc.'

It could not create any worse havoc than Nat had created in her own life, she told herself bleakly, but all she said aloud was,

'It was rough when we started out.' Nat had drawn the Rover close up to the front door at Cliff House, but even so the gusts, that seemed to come from every direction at once, reached a force that made her glad they were driving in the large, heavy car, that was not so prone to a buffeting from the elements as her own small runabout. She raised apprehensive eyes to his face.

'Don't worry, the Town Hall's sturdy enough to withstand any wind, swinging or otherwise,' he laughed away her fears, and reassured, Dee turned to answer Hugh's enquiry about her uncle, and listened as the talk turned, inevitably to ships and the sea, an inescapable subject in a maritime gathering.

'It isn't often we see a tug of the size of the *Sea Wind* in this harbour, Mr Archer.' Hugh's wife chatted happily, unselfconsciously friendly, inoffensively curious. Dee stiffened. Surely now Nat would mention his reason for coming to Penzyn, and tell them he would shortly be going away again, and why? It would be so easy for him to say,

'I'm going on a two-year round-the-world trip for —— magazine, so I thought I'd call in and see the family before I left.'

If he talked about his plans, she could ask him about them, discuss them with him naturally, without seeming curious. Her nervous fingers twisted the fringe ends of the stole into tight bands, and untwisted them again when they cut into her palms.

'There's no work for a big tug in a harbour of this size,' Nat smiled at the older woman. 'The little ones cope with all that's likely to arise here,' he answered casually, and the flatness of disappointment crept like a tide across Dee's newborn hope. It would have been so easy for him to tell them about his plans, so why did he not do so? she wondered miserably, but although she waited through a brief silence that seemed to last a hundred years, the expected words did not come, and instead Nat added with an oblique glance in her direction, 'there's no work—except towing stranded fishing smacks from off local mudbanks.' And he laughed.

Shocked disbelief turned her face to stone. For a moment she felt stunned. Then anger, disappointment, and bitter resentment rose together inside her like a floodtide, enveloping her, drowning her.

'He said that on purpose, to turn the others' interest away from his own affairs!' Without a second thought, he had used her, humiliated her, used her own careless action, that he must know she wanted desperately to forget ever happened, as a joke to serve his own purpose. The others saw the humour of it, but Dee did not. Laughter rose round her, friendly, sympathetic laughter, but the sound of it rasped at her raw pride like sandpaper.

'I hate you!'

Her eyes said it for her. They had to, because her lips

felt stiff, incapable of coherent speech, unable to form the torrent of angry words that rose to the tip of her tongue. The gathering storm outside was as nothing to the storm his careless words aroused within her. It turned her eyes black with passion, and her cheeks first scarlet and then as white as the flower that adorned her shoulder.

'How could you?' She found her voice at last, but it was only a whisper, her throat was so tight she could not utter anything more, and what she said was drowned in the confusion of chatter and laughter around them. She swallowed, and tried again, but before she had managed more than one word someone thrust something into her hand. She looked down at it dazedly, and discovered it was a goblet of ice cream. Blindly she turned away from Nat, ostensibly to thank the donor. It was Hugh. If it had been Nat who gave it to her, she thought furiously, she would have flung it back in his face, just as she longed to tear the white carnation from off her shoulder and fling that back at him, too.

'I'll always hate the smell of carnations.' She vented her pent-up feelings on the innocent flower, because in a crowded room the ethics of civilised behaviour forbade that she should vent them on Nat. The silver goblet was as cold as the ice it contained, as cold as her heart felt inside her. The shock of it in her hand steadied her, bringing her back to her surroundings and the need to appear outwardly normal, not to let the others, and particularly Nat, suspect that her heart broke inside her, her world lay in ruins about her silver-shod feet, that felt as if they would never dance again.

She took a mouthful of the ice cream, unwilling to offend Hugh, but if dust and ashes were the opposite of ambrosia, that was what it tasted like, she decided wretchedly, and inconspicuously slid the rest of it untouched on to a nearby side table.

'Shall we exchange partners for this dance, Mr Archer?'

Hugh smiled at her, seeking Nat's permission even as he held out his arms towards her, and she longed to cry out angrily,

'I'll be only too glad to change partners. You don't need to ask Nat's permission. Because he brought me here, it doesn't mean he owns me.'

She longed to strike out, to humiliate Nat as much as he had humiliated her. But instead she smiled at the fishing skipper, and bent her attention to following his less than expert lead across the floor, all the while achingly conscious that Nat followed with Hugh's wife on his arm, and apparently his whole attention on something the friendly little woman was saying to him. His head was bent in a listening attitude, his expression intent, as if he had already forgotten his previous partner, and was as happy with the exchange as Dee tried to convince herself she was, too.

The music changed, the M.C. called out an 'excuse me' dance, and Hugh was whisked away from her by a bright-faced girl with auburn hair and a happy smile. Dee wondered, dully, what it was like to feel happy, wondered if she ever would again, and tried to force her dragging feet to keep time to her new partner, who two minutes later was himself claimed by someone else, and she was left stranded and bewildered in the middle of the dance floor, among a noisy kaleidoscope of movement and colour, not knowing which way to go, where to turn. . . .

'We've both been deserted, it seems.'

A short time ago she would have regarded it as a good omen. Now it took all her willpower not to pull away from Nat's arms, to run from him to anyone, anywhere, so long as she need not dance with him again.

'Did you *have* to tell them about rescuing me from the mudbank?' She had not meant to let him know she cared. She steeled herself against the feel of his arms, the touch of his hand, but she discovered that even the strength of steel was not enough, and she called on the burning anger inside her to reinforce her defences. 'Did you *have* to?' she flared.

'I didn't tell them, they already knew. Hugh was on board the tug when we came out for you, remember?' His voice was mildly amused, and it was all that was needed to light the taper of her pent-up fury.

'Just because you didn't want to talk about your trip round the world,' she cried accusingly, 'because you didn't want to tell them about your wretched commission for that magazine,' she could not remember the name of the magazine, and she no longer cared, 'you used me to sidetrack their attention. You didn't care. . . .' She choked into silence. She had not meant to tell him she knew of his proposed trip, either, but she could not stop herself. It was out now, and there was nothing she could do about it.

'Hugh and his wife already know about my trip,' he began, and she interrupted him angrily,

'You told them about it, but you didn't tell me.' It was childish, unreasonable, and she could not help herself. She felt bitterly resentful that Nat should tell the fishing skipper and his wife, and not mention it to her. And then the moment she said it she could have bitten her tongue for uttering the words, because they betrayed that she minded, and she did not want him to know.

'I didn't need to tell them,' Nat contradicted her mildly. 'Hugh's wife takes the magazine, she'd already read the article for herself.' His eyes narrowed, watching her, with a great effort of will she tried to make her face expressionless, indifferent. 'It's public knowledge, once it's in print.'

Was that why he had not spoken of it to her? Because he assumed she would have read it for herself, that she already knew? Perhaps, she caught her breath as the thought struck her, perhaps he had even wondered why she had not brought up the subject while they were together. He might think she did not care. . . . The possibility was unbearable, and she trembled, hating the silent gulf that lay between them, searching for a means to bridge it, and in the crowded ballroom, finding none.

'Come and say hello to the family.'

She had a brief moment of hope as she shook hands with Nat's brothers and their wives. Surely now the talk would turn to his journey? If she fought shy of mentioning it, his family would have no such inhibitions. But the two older couples, more than a generation older than Nat, she realised with a sense of shock, and so very different, the two older couples seemed interested only in their own children and their juvenile sayings and doings.

'There's the journey home,' she comforted herself. 'We'll be on our own, in the car. We can talk then.' She danced through the steps of the last waltz, dreaming in Nat's arms, hardly aware of her surroundings, or the music, her mind totally absorbed in trying to decide how to broach the subject, what she would say, and what Nat would reply. It was Hugh who pricked her bubble this time. Inoffensive, kindly Hugh, who did not know that he trampled heavy-footed across her dreams.

'I've got a puncture,' he announced ruefully, as they stood in the gusty darkness on the Town Hall steps. 'The rear offside tyre's as flat as a pancake. Go inside in the warm for a few minutes, while I get out the spare,' he told his wife.

'Don't bother with changing the wheel tonight,' Nat spoke up instantly. 'I'll drop you both at home, and you can come back and deal with your tyre tomorrow, in the daylight. You'll ruin your dress shirt if you try to change the wheel in the dark,' he added practically.

The two men sat together in the front of the Rover, and Dee sat with Hugh's wife in the back.

'There'll be more room for your dresses, they won't get crumpled in the back.' And Nat shut the doors on them, then said later over his shoulder to Dee, after he had put down the fishing skipper and his wife outside their own front door and got back behind the wheel himself,

'It isn't worth your changing seats now, it's only another half mile to Cliff House.'

It was worth it to her, she thought wistfully, even if it was not worth it to Nat. But half a mile was not enough distance to talk in.

'I'll ask him into the house for a last cup of coffee,' she consoled herself. In the drawing room, on their own, in the intimacy of the dying firelight, they could talk together, and all would be well.

'It looks as if your people are waiting up for you.'

The lights in the downstairs windows of Cliff House blazed a bright welcome, and a roaring fire greeted them both as her uncle ushered them into the warm drawing room.

'You shouldn't have waited up for me.' Dee swallowed sick disappointment, and hoped her uncle would blame the wind for the tears of frustration that welled up in her eyes, despite her best efforts to fight them back. 'You should be in bed,' she scolded him.

'I've had enough of bed to last me for a lifetime,' the doughty mariner growled. 'And besides,' he excused himself, 'your aunt couldn't rest, knowing you were driving along the cliff road, and the wind's rising fit to blow the house away.'

'Come and sit down, I've made some coffee, and there's cake. . . .' Her aunt fussed with cups and saucers, and Dee felt herself stifled, trapped. At any other time she would have enjoyed the feeling of being cossetted, but now she longed to shout at them both,

'Leave me alone! Please, leave me alone. . . .'

She meant, leave her alone with Nat.

But amid the domestic busyness of handing round coffee and cake, her silent plea went unheard, and the agony in her eyes unnoticed, and she curled tense fingers round her cup, heedless of the burning heat of it against her flesh, and swallowed her sobs with her coffee. The drink gave her an excuse for monosyllables in reply to her relatives' kindly questions as to whether she had enjoyed the evening.

Had she?

She asked the same question of herself. Could she in truth say she had enjoyed an evening that had torn her pride into shreds and left her heart in shards about her feet? She bit into a cake she did not want, and used a full mouth as an excuse to allow Nat to answer for her,

'It was a very pleasant evening. It was a pity you couldn't be there.'

Did he mean he had enjoyed himself, or was he just being polite? Or, her heart misgave her, did Nat mean he wished her uncle had been able to come instead, and so save him from the boring duty of going in his place? Of escorting herself....

'It'll make a nice send-off for your trip round the world,' her aunt smiled, and plied him with more cake, and Dee nearly choked on her own as Nat launched into a discussion with the elderly couple about his coming journey. He talked as freely to them as he had to Hugh and his wife, but not to herself.

She listened in numb silence as he chatted on. Technical talk with the veteran sailor, of victualling, and things they called drafts, and the depths of waters in various harbours round the world, details of which went over Dee's head because she did not understand them. Exciting talk with her enthralled aunt, of fascinating people and faraway places, to which Dee listened, equally enthralled, and at the same time bitter in the knowledge that Nat had not talked so with her when they were alone together. To Dee herself he merely said, when at last he rose to go,

'Goodnight, Dee.'

His face, his voice, were alike expressionless. She did not answer him because she could not. Tears blocked her throat, and denied her speech. Helplessly she raised her face to his, her eyes mutely beseeching, but he did not respond. He made no attempt to kiss her goodnight. Reason argued that he could not very well do so with her uncle and aunt present, but the omission hurt, as sharp as the pain that came with the thought,

'Perhaps he's glad we're not alone, so that he needn't bother to kiss me, so that he needn't pretend. . . .'

But not nearly so sharp as the realisation that came afterwards, when at last she shut the door of her own room behind her, and was blessedly alone, with only the wild beating of the gathering storm hurtling itself against her window panes, echoing the tempo of her own disturbed mind, as wild as the beating of her sorely tried heart as it dawned upon her that while Nat had discussed his coming journey with such seeming freedom, he had carefully not mentioned the actual date when he intended to sail. Frantically she searched her memory, desperate to prove herself wrong, but each word he had spoken was emblazoned on her mind in letters of fire, and she knew it was impossible for her to forget such a vital detail.

Did he plan to sail next month? Next week? Or—she gave a tiny moan of despair, and sat down abruptly on the side of the bed, her legs trembling so much that they refused to hold her. She shivered, and pulled her dressing jacket closer about her shoulders with fingers that shook, so that she gave up trying to tie the bright ribbons— Or was he planning to sail tomorrow, on the morning tide? Was tonight the last time she would ever see him?

When he had said, 'Goodnight, Dee,' did he mean, 'Goodbye'?

CHAPTER NINE

'I'VE gone into Penzyn,' Dee scribbled hastily on the back of an old envelope; she could not wait to look out a piece of writing paper. 'We've run out of cake,' she wrote, and shook her head at the feebleness of her own excuse, but it was the only one her sleep deprived mind felt capable of. She added, 'Be back later. Dee,' and propped her message up against the side of the kitchen kettle. It was the first utensil her uncle would look for when he came downstairs, to make his early morning cup of tea.

Silently Dee closed the kitchen door behind her, secure in the knowledge that her aunt and uncle would sleep on for a while, taking their accustomed eight hours, which meant they would not be down until after nine o'clock, since Nat did not leave Cliff House until long after one that morning.

'I must see him, just once more. I can't let him go away like this, without a word.' She had not even said 'goodnight' when they parted, she had not spoken to him at all. The memory had tormented her through the long sleepless hours until daylight, as savage as the shrieking wind that tore at her now. She paused, hesitating, as the force of the gust almost knocked her off her feet.

'I *must* see him. I'll never have another chance.' She gritted her teeth, ducked, and battled her way to where the Mini stood parked against the side of the house. The temporary physical battering she endured in the process was as nothing to what the mental battering would be if she missed him, and that would go on for ever. 'If he intends to sail today, the tide's at full just after eleven o'clock,' she remembered Hugh remarking on it the night before. She did not stop to question whether Nat would put to sea in such a storm. Her tormented mind was only capable of concentrating on one thing, and nothing else mattered. Her only object was to find Nat.

Even that, she found, had to take second place when she ran the car out on to the cliff road and faced it towards Penzyn. She was only a short distance from the house when a gust of such velocity roared in from the sea that it stopped the Mini in its tracks, and, even at that height on top of the cliffs, showered the windscreen with spray, blotting out the road, the sea, the landscape generally in a blinding sheet of spindrift. It was as if the storm, having cowed everything else before it, saw another victim on which to vent its wrath, and pounced.

For a brief, heart-stopping minute, fear took Dee by the throat as the car rocked violently, then the gust roared on, the Mini righted itself, and she flicked the screen wipers into action. Her confidence returned somewhat when the world appeared through the windscreen once more.

'If the Mini will stand that, it'll stand anything,' she muttered out loud, and the sound of her own voice further restored her self-assurance. She felt surprised that the car still stood on its four wheels; she had heard tales of cars being blown over the cliffs into the sea. But, realisation calmed her still further, this wind was blowing from the direction of the sea, towards the land.

'So it can't blow me into the water.' She let out a long, relieved breath. 'The worst it can do will be to blow me into the hedge.' Cautiously she slid the gears into action and set the car rolling again slowly. Even a battered Mini was preferable to not seeing Nat ever again, she reminded herself numbly, and if she crawled along until the road dipped into shelter behind the cliffs, she would still be in time. She glanced at her watch. It was only half past nine now, the tide would not be full for another two hours, and Nat would not take the big tug out until the water was high. Even then she did not question that he would take it out at all, in such a storm unless it was vitally necessary. It did not occur to her beleagured mind that on a journey which was to take two years, one day's delay was unlikely to make much difference.

The next gust hit the car from behind, and she remembered Nat's words, '... an oscillating wind, swinging between two compass points.'

'One gust pulls, and the other pushes,' she discovered an element of grim humour in the situation. It helped, she found, as the valiant little vehicle staggered under repeated body blows, making her arms ache and her nerves scream with the strain of keeping it on the road.

'Thank goodness there's no traffic about.' It struck her as odd, at nearly ten o'clock in the morning, that there was no traffic about, but she took grateful advantage of the unusual, and steered a careful course in the middle of the road, which entered Penzyn from the rear of the town.

'I'll park in the Town Hall car park,' Dee decided, heeding her uncle's oft-repeated warning,

'When there's a wind from the sea, don't park on the sea front. You risk getting sand in your carburettors.'

What sand would do to her carburettors she had no idea, and since she had just paid a large sum of money to have them attended to, she did not want to find out. With a sigh of relief she drew in next to the only other car in the park. Two men doing something to the rear of it started to straighten up as she got out of her seat.

'Miss Lawrence?' It was Hugh. She had forgotten his car would still be there because of the punctured tyre. He stared at her as if she was some kind of apparition, started to say, 'Whatever are you doing, out in this weather?' when his attention was diverted by the second man, who rose to his feet just behind Hugh.

'What on earth are you doing here?'

It was Nat. And there was no doubt he was furiously angry. With one stride he stood over Dee, glaring down at her with a scowl that resembled the elements in its ferocity. 'Why have you come into Penzyn?' he demanded harshly. 'Is something wrong at Cliff House? Are your uncle and aunt ill?'

'No, nothing's wrong, they're both perfectly all right.' Why should there be anything wrong? she wondered, taken aback by his behaviour. His leavetaking the evening before had been civil enough, so why should he shout at her now? He had no need to raise his voice all that much, the bulk of the Town Hall sheltered them from the worst effects of the storm. By normal standards it was still unbearably rough in the car park, but compared to the conditions on the cliff road, it was a haven of peace. It had seemed like a haven of peace, until she encountered Nat.

'If there's no emergency, what in the name of sanity made you drive along the cliff road, drive anywhere, in a storm like this?' he shouted at her. 'The wind alone is enough to send you into orbit!' As if to emphasise his words a screaming gust whipped round the corner of the building and hit them with a force that made her stagger. It did not make Nat stagger, she noticed crossly. He swayed, bending to the strength of it, but he stood his ground, reaching out to grasp her by the arm as she stumbled and might have lost her balance but for his grip.

'There's no need to grab me like that, I'm not a bale of cargo!' she cried, stung to anger herself by the bruising force of his fingers round her arm. They hurt, but not so much as his touch bruised her heart. . . . The feel of them reinforced her agony of the sleepless night before, and melted her resolve to remain calm when they met.

'Thanks again, Mr Archer, reckon I'll be off now.' Hugh nodded to Dee politely. 'Miss Lawrence.' He took his leave of them both and vanished, but it was doubtful if either Dee or Nat saw him go; they were solely occupied with one another.

'What brought you into Penzyn today, of all days?' Nat demanded to know.

'I can come into Penzyn just when I like!' What right had he to question her comings and goings? she asked herself furiously. She had come into Penzyn to see him, but she could not tell him so. She could not even ask him, now, if she had made her journey in vain. 'If this is his attitude, I wish I hadn't bothered,' she thought wrathfully. A game on the rug with Skip would have been far preferable to the battle of driving along the cliff road. Even now, the thought of the return journey made her blanch.

'Well?' He waited for her explanation, grim, uncompromising.

'I came. . . .' She had no intention of letting him know why she came. She did not care, any longer, whether he would sail with the morning tide or not. She did not care when he sailed, or to where, she told herself, and wished he would loose her arm, then perhaps she could persuade herself with more conviction, when the feel of his fingers holding her did not send strange thrills through her that set her blood pounding in a way that matched the wild beating of the storm.

'I came because we'd run out of cake.' She blurted out the only explanation that came into her head, the one she had given in her note to her relatives. It sounded even more feeble now, than it had done when she scribbled it on the back of the used envelope.

'You came to buy cake? *Cake?*' He stared down at her, incredulous, disbelieving. 'You drove through a Force Ten gale, to buy cake?' Words failed him at the sheer unexpectedness of her answer. He stared down at her for an electrifying minute as if he thought she might have taken leave of her senses, and his grip on her arm momentarily slackened. Dee took instant advantage of it.

'Yes, cake,' she thrust back at him angrily, and with a quick twist freed herself from his hold. 'I'm going to the bakers now. And I don't need you to take me there!' She flung away from him and ignominiously took to her heels. If she did not run he would see the tears that scalded her eyes and ran down her cheeks.

'Dee, come back!'

She ignored his shout. She knew what it felt like, to shout 'Come back,' she thought with bitter humour. All too often in the past few weeks she herself had shouted, 'Skip, come back!' and now Nat should know what it felt like, she told herself vindictively, to shout orders, and to have those orders ignored.

'Dee....'

'Shout as loud as you want to, I'll go where I please,' she muttered rebelliously, and ran round the corner of the Town Hall. The baker's shop was on the promenade, not far away from the Town Hall, whose imposing front looked out over the holiday beach.

'Dee!'

She skidded to a halt, appalled at the sight that greeted her along the sea front. The wind tore at her, whipped her clothes against her body, plastering her lightweight mac flat round her, so cold that she might not have had a windproof on. It blew her breath back into her nostrils, stifling her. It whipped her hair round her eyes, blinding her. Deafened by the roar of the wind and the water, terrified by the huge waves crashing over the promenade, the road awash with water a foot deep, she turned back on her tracks, dazed.

'I didn't know it was as bad as this.'

'Surely you must have seen, from the cliff road?' Nat caught up with her, caught her to him, and held her, blessedly secure. 'The force of the wind alone should have told you what it was like by the shore, that it wasn't safe for you to venture out in the car.' He was angry, furiously angry, she could feel the force of his fury through the hard, relentless grip of his arms, but even Nat's anger was as nothing to the demonic force of wrath that drove the running tide like a mighty battering ram against the sea wall, great breakers of water house high that smashed across the normally busy promenade like an invading army. Belatedly it dawned upon Dee that the baker's shop had shutters tight across its windows. So had the hotels facing the sea front. Storm shutters.

'If one of those waves catches you, you won't stand a chance.'

'I didn't know....' She had been too occupied with driving, too obsessed with her overriding need to reach Nat, for the full import of the storm's savagery to penetrate her mind. Now, the consequences of her impulsive action dawned upon her fully for the first time, and she shuddered.

'I'll go back home.' She tried to pull away from him.

'You'll do nothing of the kind,' he told her masterfully. 'It isn't safe for you to drive in this wind, particularly in your little runabout.'

'My little runabout stood the journey here as well as your car would have done.' Her pride was stung by his contemptuous reference to her gallant little vehicle, and she closed her mind to the terror that gripped her at the thought of the return journey. 'I've got to go home. There's nowhere else to go.' Only with Nat, and contrarily now she did not want to stay with Nat. She wanted to flee from him, hide where he could not reach her. She felt more afraid of his anger than she did of the storm, and wished too late she had not come. 'I've got to....'

'Listen!'

She felt him tense, saw his head go up, listening, searching for a new sound that rose above the fury of the storm.

'What is it?' The latest gust passed by, and in the vacuum of comparative quiet, an unearthly wail arose, floating across the beleaguered town like the voice of doom. It cut across the anger and the defiance, put aside the quarrelling, and left only her frightened question,

'What is it?'

It gathered strength to compete with the noise of the

wind and the crash of the waves, and raised Dee's eyes, wide with terror, to Nat's face.

'It's the siren to call out the lifeboat men. There must be a ship in trouble, somewhere out there.'

She felt the anger drain from him, dissipated by this new, sudden emergency that took his whole attention, took him in spirit far away from her. The vibrant force of his hold upon her slackened, and although his arms remained around her she felt as if, to Nat, she was no longer there.

'Nat, come back to me. Come back. . . .'

She raised imploring eyes to his face, and her heart wept. His anger was better than this. But he did not notice her looking up at him, he did not look down, his face was turned away from her towards the sea, his thoughts on the cry for help that rose from somewhere out among the wild water, and echoed in the eerie wailing that went on and on, until she longed to bury her face in Nat's jacket, close her ears against the awful banshee dirge. Her own heart sent out a cry for help, but it had no loud voiced siren to reinforce it, and her cry went unheard.

'I wonder whereabouts. . . .'

He spoke more to himself than to her, then added in a louder voice,

'Come and stand in the shelter of the doorway for a minute or two, I want to see the lifeboat go out, I want to know in which direction they're heading.' He drew her with him into the deep Town Hall doorway, out of the buffeting of the wind.

'D'you think it's one of the Archer line ships?' It had not occurred to her that it might be one of his father's vessels in trouble. How awful, if it was someone he knew.

'I doubt it. So far as I know, our people aren't expecting any of the fleet back until the middle of next week.'

So it was a strange vessel. There was some relief in that for her, but she felt with quick intuition, none for Nat.

None for any seaman watching, who had shared the perils, and knew what the cost might be.

'Let them get there in time,' she prayed silently, and crept closer under the shelter of Nat's arm, forgetful for the moment of her need to hide from him. She had watched the lifeboat launched before, but never in conditions like this. No sooner had it touched the water than it disappeared completely in the trough of a huge wave.

'It'll capsize. Why do they go out?' she cried. 'No one can survive in seas like this!'

'The lifeboat's made to right itself.'

'But the men?' Dee sobbed. She did not care about the lifeboat. Lifeboats could be replaced. 'What about the men?'

'They know their job,' he answered her quietly, his eyes still on the water.

'They're risking their lives,' she protested.

He looked down at her then, and she could have cried aloud at the sombre light in his black eyes, a light that was not for her, but a thing apart, that locked her out, cut her off from him more surely even than his anger.

'He wishes he was out there with them,' she realised, aghast. 'He wishes he was with the lifeboat, going to the help of that ship, instead of having to stand here on the shore with me, looking on.'

'They're seamen, Dee.'

As if that answered everything, she thought frantically, and longed to shout at him, to beat against him with her fists, to make him understand.

'They're husbands, fathers, sons and brothers. They're all those things as well, not just seamen.'

The tears coursed down her cheeks uncontrolled, and she shivered violently within the circle of his arms.

'It's time you went indoors, you'll catch a chill.'

As if a chill mattered! A boatful of men faced unimaginable dangers, and Nat bothered about her catching a chill. She caught an hysterical breath.

'They haven't overturned—look.' He turned her round, forcing her to look out across the water. 'They're still safe.'

Safe would hardly be the word Dee would have used, but at least the lifeboat was still afloat. And making way against the waves, she realised incredulously, unable to believe that she could still actually see the tiny cockleshell lifted on the heads of combers so huge they seemed capable of drowning the town, and then flung down into the troughs, as a child flings down a toy in a tantrum, only to rise again on the head of the next comber....

'Why do they do it?' she whispered in awe. 'Why do any of them go out there at all? It's safe, behind the harbour bar....'

She felt him pause, then, felt his stillness, and his eyes rake her face. Questioning her courage? She did not care. She felt shaken out of all control by the effects of her drive along the cliff road; by Nat's anger, and his unexpected concern in case she should catch a chill.

'Why do they do it?' she cried at him desperately. 'Why?'

But all he said in reply was,

'It's time you went indoors, out of the storm. I'll take you to Hugh's house. I can phone from there and tell your people you're safe.'

Suddenly she felt too weary to protest any more. It had not occurred to her that her aunt and uncle might be worried about her safety. She had not given a thought for herself until now. And sitting beside the fire in Hugh's own armchair half an hour later, which the fishing skipper pushed closer to the hearth to warm her frozen feet, and his wife plied her with hot cocoa to bring some life back into her numbed body, she listened as if in a dream while Nat phoned Cliff House and she heard him say,

'Yes, for cake, would you believe! No, she hasn't got any, the shop was closed. They're all shuttered against the storm. Yes, don't worry, I'll keep her here with Hugh and his wife, until it's safe for her to drive back.'

Why couldn't he say, 'I'll keep her here with me'?

Dee did not remember dozing off. She only remembered feeling warm, and secure, as if for a brief space of time she had crept out of the storm of emotion that rocked her, and found shelter behind some personal harbour bar, a cosy, safe feeling, made up of the warm fire in front of her, the hot cocoa inside her, and most of all by the sight of Nat, sitting drinking his own mug of cocoa in the chair opposite to her own. Like Darby and Joan, was her last conscious thought before her heavy lids closed and she succumbed to the twin drugs of warmth and weariness, and slept.

The telephone bell roused her. Vaguely in the distance she could hear its sharp, persistent summons, and wondered irritably why someone did not answer it. Then it stopped abruptly, and she heard Hugh's voice say,

'Aye, he's here with us now. It's for you, Mr Archer. It's the coastguard.'

She came fully awake then. Nat was gone from the chair opposite to her, but he must be still in the room if Hugh spoke to him. She sat up and looked round the side of the big wing chair in time to see him take the telephone receiver from Hugh's hand. He had to stoop, she noticed, to save bumping his head on the beams of the low cottage ceiling. Hugh was tall, and he could stand upright, but not Nat. She had not noticed, before, how very tall Nat was.

She studied his face, intent on the chatter of speech coming through the receiver. She saw him tense, and frown, then his expression cleared and he said in relieved tones,

'So they got the crew off safely? All of them?' The answer must have been in the affirmative, because he smiled and added, 'Thank goodness they got there in time!'

'He must be talking about the ship that was in distress, the one the lifeboat went out to help,' she surmised. It was a wonder the ship's crew, or the lifeboat men, had returned at all, she thought, remembering the comparatively tiny boat, and the mountainous size of the waves. Her thoughts stopped short as Nat continued,

'Drifting, you said? Which way?' The receiver chattered for a moment and then went silent, and Nat frowned. 'Which side of Penzyn, the harbour or—oh, towards the beach side. I see.' There was a pause, then he added consideringly, as if replying to a question, 'Yes, the *Sea Wind*'s capable of holding the ship steady, even in a blow like this. The difficulty will be to get a grapple to hold fast. It'll have to be a grapple, if there's no crew left on board to tie a line. How badly is she listing?' He listened for a second or two longer, then said decisively, 'I'm on my way. It'll take me about fifteen minutes to get to the harbour, and we can be ready to set sail in another twenty from then. I'll keep the wireless open and stand by. Contact me when you've got some more directions.'

Dee listened, stunned. Nat was actually contemplating an attempt to take the foundering vessel in tow, as calmly as if he was the garage foreman making plans to tow in a broken-down car! Her own calm fled as the implications of the conversation dawned upon her, and she jumped to her feet impulsively, horror and disbelief making her almost incoherent as she cried,

'You can't put to sea in a storm like this! Don't let him, Hugh,' she turned desperately to the fishing skipper, 'it's crazy!' She felt sick as she remembered the lifeboat, but that, at least, was built to right itself if it capsized. Tugs were not. 'It's madness!' She caught at Nat's jacket as he turned from replacing the receiver on its rest, and her hands tried to shake him, tried to make him understand. 'It's madness!' she panted, and realised despairingly that she might as well try to shake the Rock of Gibraltar as try to turn him from his intended course.

'It's worth a try. It just might succeed.'

So he had doubts about its success, even before he started. She could hardly believe that he really meant what he said. And *he* had shouted at *her* for daring to drive through the storm....

'It isn't worth risking your life for.' Terror goaded her into fury, her own inability to get through to him turning to anger, that he should torment her so. 'It isn't as if there are any people aboard,' she made one last desperate attempt to convince him. 'All you'll be rescuing is an empty ship.' Ships could be replaced, people could not. Without conscious thought she put herself in front of him, between Nat and the door, as if she would prevent him from going out by sheer force, if necessary. She did not stop to reason that her own tiny figure had no hope of stopping Nat, even if she tried. She did not think of anything, except that he intended to put to sea in a gale the force of which she had never experienced before. She had felt his yearning to be out with the lifeboat crew, even as he stood beside her in the Town Hall doorway, watching the rescue craft battle its way out to sea, and now....

'The waves came in like rolling graves.'

One of her uncle's fishermen had used the expression to describe the storm in which her relative had been injured, and surely the one that was blowing now was far worse? She drew in a deep, shuddering breath, and forced her tight throat to let her voice come through.

'Don't go, Nat. Please, don't go,' she implored him huskily, and her heart looked out of her eyes. Unconsciously she reached out her hands to him, beseeching him. 'Don't go....' For a brief moment she thought she had won. A strange, unreadable expression flicked across his face as his eyes met and locked with her own, unfathomable, heart-stopping. He reached out his own hands and put them on her shoulders, and put her gently but firmly aside, and said,

'I have to go, Dee. It's the cargo....'

She stared up at him, shock and disbelief draining the colour from her face. And then anger surged up in her, passionate anger such as she had never known before, thrusting aside her fear, her love, and venting itself in hot, accusing words, wild words that poured from her, tumbling off her tongue like molten fire, accusing, condemning,

'So that's it? It's the cargo that matters to you—you're going out for the salvage, not the ship. You'd risk your life to get salvage money!' Bitter contempt hung in her tones, and his face whitened, matching her own, but she did not care. She hated him for putting her on the rack like this, tearing her apart with fear for his life when all he cared about was the salvage money. His hands tightened on her shoulders, gripping her with bruising force, and a small, detached part of her mind noticed a muscle twitching, twitching, at the point of his jaw. Vaguely she remembered seeing it twitch like that once before, but she could not remember when. It was the only sign of emotion in his rock-hard face—that, and the searing anger in his eyes. He glared down at her through a tight silence, and she felt as if twin rods of fire speared her to the spot.

'Nat, I. . . .' She did not know what she wanted to say. Whatever it was, her paralysed tongue refused to say it, just as her paralysed limbs refused to let her obey her heart and run after him to the door when he put her from him, roughly pushing her out of his path.

'I'll come along with you, Mr Archer.'

Surely not Hugh as well? She stared mutely at the fishing skipper's wife, waiting for her protest, but although the older woman's eyes showed the same anguish as her own, she remained silent, compliant, accepting the decision of her man.

'Well, I don't,' Dee told herself stormily. But Nat was not her man, and before she could say anything more he spoke directly to the fishing skipper, ignoring Dee.

'No, Hugh. You must stay here, and stand by the telephone for us. This is a job for single men.'

For a brief second Nat's eyes raked Dee's face, then they passed on. He nodded to the fisherman's wife, said, 'See you,' to Hugh, and without another glance in Dee's direction he closed the door behind him and was gone.

'What does he mean, a job for single men?'

Through the daze of anger, his choice of expression tugged at her mind, and she stared at Hugh, uncomprehending. Was there something else behind his words, something she did not understand? Perhaps, she caught her breath, and her heart froze with a new fear, perhaps there was some special danger that Nat had not mentioned, but that Hugh, being a seaman, would know about?

Or, and her anger returned, armouring her against fear, or were his words merely aimed as a barb at herself, letting her know he was glad that he was single, that he could go where he liked, and do what he pleased, and no one, least of all herself, had the right to ask him to do otherwise?

CHAPTER TEN

DEE slept the night in the spare bedroom at Hugh's cottage. Sleep was a misnomer. Rather did she pace the floor of the tiny room, half a dozen paces from the window to the door, and half a dozen back again, she counted each one until she felt like a lion she had seen years before at a zoo, pacing the floor of a cage.

'If only I knew! If only I could see. . . .'

But the bedroom window faced inland, and she could not go downstairs to look out of the windows that faced towards the sea, for fear of disturbing her host and hostess. If she did, it was doubtful whether she would see anything through the inky blackness of the storm anyway, but there might be some comfort in trying.

'He might not have taken the *Sea Wind* out, after all. He only said he would stand by.'

But that thought brought her no consolation, either.

'It's worth a try,' Nat had said. It was a challenge, like a dare to a small boy, she thought, trying in vain to whip up renewed anger to armour her against encroaching fear. But through the long hours of tempestuous darkness the fear won, tearing at her imagination, destroying her defences, until at last, defeated, she dropped her face into her hands and sobbed out loud the only thing in the world that really mattered.

'I love you, Nat. I love you. . . .'

Faint light filtered through the curtains before she eventually dropped into an exhausted doze. The light had turned to sunshine when she awoke. She blinked and opened her eyes, then became aware, faintly from somewhere below, of the cheerful bustle of household sounds, and, she sniffed, the smell of frying bacon. And something else. Something that was not there, rather than something that was. She frowned, unable to place the thing that was missing.

'The noise! There's no noise.'

She jumped to her feet and fled to the window, thrusting aside the curtains with eager hands. Outside, the sun-bathed garden smiled brightly back at her. The bushes stood upright, unmoving, serene as if the storm had never bent them flat.

'The wind's dropped—the storm's over!' It was as if a great weight had been lifted from the world, from her own weary shoulders. She ran downstairs with hasty steps, heedless of the danger of a ricked ankle on the twisting, narrow stairway as her feet flew kitchenwards. 'The storm's over!' She burst through the door, unable to contain the good news.

'Aye,' Hugh's wife took the wonder more calmly, and turned with a smile from the stove. 'The wind dropped round about dawn. There's still quite a swell running, from all accounts, but that'll die down by and by. The worst seems to be over.'

'Where's Hugh?' Dee longed to ask, 'Where's Nat?' but the words stuck in her throat and refused to be said.

'He's gone down to the beach to try and find out what's happened.'

'He doesn't know whether the *Sea Wind* went out last night, then?' It had to be asked. She clenched her hands under the tablecloth, dreading the answer.

'No, he's had no news since Nat left us last night. The coastguard hasn't phoned. I expect Hugh will be back when he's found out what they decided to do. We'll know, by and by,' Hugh's wife said comfortably.

Everything seemed to be happening by and by, Dee thought impatiently. She longed to cry out, 'I want to know *now*,' but the motherly little woman was putting a plate of bacon and eggs in front of her and saying,

'Have a bite of breakfast before you go to collect your car, you had nothing for supper last night.'

And there was no chance to ask any more questions, only to try and tackle the breakfast that to Dee's dismayed eyes looked as if it could have served six people instead of one. She did not want any breakfast. She had not wanted anything for supper the night before. She only wanted Nat. But to please Hugh's wife she somehow managed to plod through the food in front of her, and wished, as her aching throat attempted to swallow, that Skip was with her to help her out. But Hugh did not own a dog, and she had to cope on her own, and afterwards politeness demanded she should remain and help with the washing up, while her impatient nerves screamed at her to run from the room, run from the house, speed to the shore to find Nat, and tell him she did not mean the words she shouted at him the night before. Tell him instead that she loved him. . . .

At last she was free to go. But which way? She stood irresolute at the cottage gate. If Nat had not gone out at all, he would still be on the tug in the harbour. If he had gone out, and completed his mission successfully, he would still have to return to the harbour, as the water on the beach side of the town would not be high enough to take the *Sea Wind* until high tide, even with a heavy swell running. Dee glanced at her watch. There was over an hour to go yet, before high tide. But if Nat was still using the tug as an anchor to hold the crippled vessel from drifting any further in towards the sea front, he would be standing off the beach side of the town. She remembered him saying the boat was drifting towards the beach last night.

'I'll get the car first. That way I can go along the beach and see if the *Sea Wind*'s standing off that side of the shore. If the crippled ship's drifted close in, then they should be in sight on the horizon.' And if she had her car, it would be quicker to drive down to the harbour afterwards if the

Sea Wind was still berthed there. Her mind made up, she sped towards the sea front. 'Someone's bound to know what happened last night,' she decided. 'Even if I don't meet Hugh, someone will tell me. Everyone will be talking about the storm.' To the holidaymakers it would probably be a thrill, an added bonus of drama to their fortnightly break.

To herself? She closed her mind to what it meant to herself, and ran on, taking a short cut across the sand dunes to save herself some time. After a while she had to slow down when her breath refused to keep pace with her feet, and she climbed out of the dunes to find easier walking away from the sand, on to a side street, where she rounded a corner that led on to the sea front, and leaned against a friendly pillar box to get her breath back. She could see the whole of the beach and the promenade from where she stood. The whole of the wide, empty space of the sea.

'He's not there.'

She gulped back sick disappointment, and for a moment or two actually needed the pillar box to help her to remain upright. There was not a ship to be seen. The sea was deserted, right to the horizon. As deserted as the beach, and the promenade.

'What...?' She frowned. It was almost eerie, like some futuristic picture, in which she was the only person left in the world.

'Don't be ridiculous,' she scolded herself back to normality. Storm and fright had shaken her badly, worse than she had realised. It was high time she took herself in hand, she thought determinedly.

'If the tug's not in sight, it simply means that Nat wasn't called out after all,' she told herself practically, and pushed herself firmly off the pillar box, and forced herself to walk on, along the street. But why was the beach deserted, and the promenade? At ten o'clock in the morning it was normally crowded with playing children, sunbathing parents, donkeys, Punch and Judy shows, and ice cream vendors. Now, there was not a soul in sight. It was warm and sunny, the tide was not full yet, and the long stretch of golden sand lay invitingly open. And there was not a holidaymaker to be seen.

It was then Dee saw the ship. It was a cargo vessel, not one of the Archer line but bigger, and it lay at the other end of the beach, tipped on its side like a huge, stranded whale, pathetic in its helplessness.

'He didn't manage to get a grapple to hold, after all.' The thought flashed across her mind even as she caught sight of the shutters. She stared at them, and for some reason she felt oddly cold. The shutters were still tightly closed over the bakery windows, tightly shut on all the hotels, just the same as they had been at the height of the storm the day before. But the storm was over now.

'You can't come any further along here, miss. How did you get this far, in any case? Where have you come from?'

A uniformed patrolman stepped out in front of her from beside a Panda car, and Dee halted in her tracks.

'I came across the dunes.'

'Ah, you're a local,' the policeman guessed. 'I hadn't bargained for the locals taking a short cut. Just a minute, if you please.' He bent and spoke to his colleague in the Panda car. 'Radio back to base, and get them to close the way in over the dunes,' he commanded urgently. 'Be quick about it, in case someone else gets the same idea.' He turned back to Dee. 'I'm sorry, miss, you'll have to go back.'

'But why? What's happening? Why isn't there anybody on the beach?'

'Because we can't have sightseers getting in the way of salvage operations, that's why.'

Incredibly it was Nat's voice, Nat's figure towering over the Panda car.

'Nat!' She forgot everything but the fact that he was safe.

'So you'll have to go back, like the man said.' Nat's expression was stern, unsmiling. Remembering what she had said to him the night before? His look did not reflect her own joy at seeing him, and the smile fled from her face.

'If I've got to go back out of the way, then so must you,' she answered him sharply, resenting his tone. Really, men were insufferable! she told herself angrily. They ordered other people about as if they were so many pawns to be shifted here and there at their own pleasure. He ordered her out of the way as if she was simply a nuisance, yet no doubt he thought he had a right to remain himself, and watch whatever was going on. 'I'll go back when you do,' she told him with spirit.

'You'll go now,' he commanded her sharply, and took her arm in a firm grip.

'And I suppose you intend to remain behind and watch?' she flashed angrily. 'I suppose you think it's perfectly all right for you to stay, but not for other people?'

'I've got work to do.'

'What work?' she demanded angrily. 'Giving orders to the salvage workers, I suppose?' she asked sarcastically.

'Mr Archer's going to use his tug to tow the vessel out of reach,' the policeman began, but Nat interrupted him curtly, almost as if he did not want her to know about what he intended to do, Dee thought resentfully.

'We're going to pull the ship off the beach at high tide, and into deep water.'

'You were going to put grapples on her last night.'

'They wouldn't hold. The only one we got to grip pulled what it latched on to out of its moorings, and the line snapped.'

Cool words to describe a death-defying struggle against hopeless odds. The strain of the struggle showed fleetingly in his face as he spoke, then it was gone as she cried bitterly,

'So you lost your chance to earn salvage money last night, and now you're going to try and make up for it,' she accused him. 'You should leave the work to the local tugmen,' she told him furiously. 'The *Sea Wind*'s only a visitor here, your work is out in deep waters, not on shore. You've no right to come here and take the living out of the local men's mouths!'

She hated him for his persistent quest for salvage money, she told herself fiercely. Last night it was different, the coastguards had asked for his help, and only the *Sea Wind* could withstand the weather conditions. This morning the harbour tugs could cope well enough. Nat was virtually wresting their living from them, by taking work that was rightfully theirs.

'A little tug isn't strong enough.'

'They could use more than one. They've done it often enough before, working in tandem, and sharing the salvage money.' She scorned his excuse for the paltry thing it was.

'Leave men's work to men,' he told her in clipped tones, dismissing her right to interfere. 'The local tugs will get their payment all in good time, never fear.'

'You don't wait for your payment. You take it in kind, on the spot.' She would never forgive him for the payment he had exacted from her for towing the fishing smack off the mudbank. She turned away from him blindly, desperate to hide the welling tears that threatened to spill over if she stayed talking with him, quarrelling with him, for a moment longer. In her desperation she forgot he still held her by the arm. With a quick tightening of his grip he spun her back to face him.

'You only paid the standing charge,' he growled. 'I forgot to add the surcharge.'

The gale that had blown the night before was a zephyr compared to this. The smouldering anger that rode Nat blazed into sudden electrifying life and burned itself out in his kiss. He forced his lips down on her own with a hard, implacable pressure that scorched like living flame, a burning torch that kindled a like fire within her, rising from the ashes of her pride to glory in the pain of her own bruised lips, the crushing force of his arms that held her to him. She ceased to struggle, and with a tiny moan of surrender she raised her own arms to clasp him even closer to her, warming herself at the fire, uncaring how it burned, uncaring for the scars the burns would leave behind. This was what she had come for, the reason she had braved the storm, and Nat's anger, and would willingly do so over again if she had to. Vaguely she was aware of the two policemen, both back in the Panda car, talking into the radio, then she was aware only of herself, and of Nat—Nat—Nat.... She melted against him, resistance forgotten and anger dead, lost in a world of passionate longing that could only find fulfilment with Nat. Breathlessly she raised her lips to meet his, returning kiss for kiss, unconscious that his arms had slackened their hold upon her until he said,

'Consider the account settled. Paid in full.' He receipted it with one more punishing kiss, full on her lips, which parted in wordless agony as he gritted,

'Now do as you're told, and go right away, out of range....'

He checked himself abruptly, as if regretting that he had said so much, and thrust her from him, his hands hard against her, rejecting her. Dazedly Dee became aware of the two policemen again. They were getting out of the Panda car, turning to speak to Nat, behaving as if nothing had happened.

'Go right away, out of range.'

Out of range of what? Himself? He was a deadly marksman, she acknowledged bitterly, and she had wandered unbeknown, straight into the range of his arrow. She had become his target, and, wounded to the heart, she must escape as best she could.

'The lady can go along in the car with the driver, sir,' the first policeman spoke to Nat. 'He's going to park up on the dunes to block anyone coming into town from that direction. I've got to stay on here to keep this end of the road clear.' He smiled at Dee kindly. 'You can watch all you want to, from up on the dunes, miss. You'll be quite safe up there.'

Safely out of Nat's way.

Her heart was broken, the pain of it was well nigh unendurable, and her life lay in ruins about her feet—but,

'You can watch all you want to, from up on the dunes.'

It was like giving a child a sugar lump as a reward for swallowing nasty-tasting medicine. Her chin rose.

'I'll stay with the car.' She spoke to the policeman, not to Nat. She refused to bend to his will, she told herself stubbornly; refused to go away, right away as he ordered her to. She would remain and watch if she wanted to, albeit from a distance, with the driver of the police car.

'I do want to. I do!' her heart cried, and she steeled herself not to listen. The effort cost her an instant, throbbing pain in her temples, forerunner of a blinding headache, but she kept her head high and her pride intact.

'And where will you be in the meantime?' she asked Nat icily, and instantly answered herself before he could speak, 'down on the shore with the crippled ship, I suppose?'

'Right in one,' he answered her crisply. 'I've wasted enough time here as it is.'

So kissing her had been a waste of time. Exacting the last ounce of payment for rescuing her from the mudbank had been a waste of time. Her heart bled as his arrow twisted in the cruel wound, and she had only pride with which to staunch the flow.

'How long do you reckon, Mr Archer?' one of the policemen asked.

'Any moment now,' Nat replied. 'George is bringing the *Sea Wind* round at peak tide, he'll stand offshore while I tie the lines on the vessel, then I'll join him on board and we'll pull the ship off into mid-channel. We've got to move her at peak tide. There won't be another chance.'

'The shipping lanes are well clear,' the policeman nodded seriously. 'The coastguards have alerted all traffic likely to enter the area to stand well off for as long as necessary.'

'They're talking in riddles,' Dee thought, bewildered. Why should they have to keep the shipping lanes clear for the sake of one stranded vessel? Why should there not be another chance after peak tide? The tide came in twice a day.

'The police launch is on the radio, sir,' the second uniformed man spoke to Nat, interrupting his colleague. 'They want to know if they can give you a lift from the vessel on to the tug when you've finished.'

'Tell them no,' Nat said curtly. 'The fewer people there are about, the better.'

'Arrogant!' Dee exclaimed under her breath. He obviously thought no one but himself was capable of coping with the job.

'The *Sea Wind*'s rounding the headland now,' Nat nodded to where the big tug nosed into sight. 'I've no time to stand talking, it'll be in reach within minutes.'

No time to stand talking to her?

He turned on his heel, and without another word or another look in her direction, he strode away across the beach, making towards the foundered vessel.

'There goes a brave man.'

It was the first policeman, speaking softly, half to himself. Dee looked at him dumbly, and he added for her benefit, with a jerk of his thumb towards the wreck, 'Yon vessel's a floating bomb.'

'You mean a stranded bomb,' his colleague corrected him, without humour.

'A—bomb?' Dee looked from one to the other, her bewilderment showing in her face.

'Aye. Mr Archer didn't seem too keen to let on what he was doing while you were here, miss. But we've had to evacuate all the buildings on the sea front. It's the cargo, you see.'

That was what Nat had said, last night. 'It's the cargo....'

'It's a chemical of some kind.'

'It's ——.' His colleague spoke the almost unpronounceable word with obvious pride.

'What of it?' Dee asked abstractedly, and her mind worked with lightning speed. The speed of fear. She knew of the chemical. 'It's usually in crystal form, for safety's sake it's kept in. . . .'

'Lead containers.' The man was determined to air his knowledge, she thought, irritation mingling with mounting dread as she stared at him. She knew exactly what he was going to say next, perhaps even better than the man himself did, even though she hoped—she prayed—he would not say it. He said,

'Aye, but the containers have burst—at least, some of them have. It seems one of the bulkheads gave way in that storm last night and the containers got jostled together a bit.' It would be more than enough, Dee knew, and longed to shut her ears to what she knew must come next. 'The trouble is, the vessel got holed somehow. Mr Archer reckons it hit some submerged wreckage that had been dredged up by the storm, while the ship drifted ashore last night, and water's seeping into the hold where the chemical's been spilled.' The words had been said, and nothing could alter them.

Like a flash Dee saw again the wording in her textbook at a seminar she attended on the properties of new chemicals; saw again her own cryptic wording in her notebook.

'—— plus water equals a loud bang.'

'—— will explode if it makes contact with water.' The lecturer had put it more formally, but the result would be the same. And the stranded vessel, holed, and taking in water, carried a whole cargo of the chemical.

'That's why everywhere's still boarded up. Why the shutters are closed on the windows.' The reason for the shutters dawned on her like a douche of icy water. If the spilled chemical exploded it would set the whole cargo off, with a blast enough to collapse the buildings on the promenade like a pack of cards. Dee felt an hysterical desire to laugh. Keeping the shutters closed was about as useless as trying to check a charging elephant with a straw!

'Nat! Nat, come back....' It was her turn to call, 'Come back!' now. Her breath sobbed in her throat as she spun away from the startled policeman and fled after Nat, her feet carrying her across the sand on wings of fear. 'Nat, come back!' Her voice was hoarse as she cried out, as loudly as her panting breath would allow her.

'Nat!'

'Here, miss, you can't go on the beach. It isn't safe. Come back!' The policeman was at it now, Dee thought hysterically, and ran on.

'You can't go on the beach, miss. I told you, it isn't safe.' The young policeman was in better training than Dee. A noted local sprinter, in the peak of physical condition, he soon outdistanced her.

'Let me go!' She struggled frantically to break his hold. 'The vessel might explode. I must warn Nat. He's heard me—look, he's turning round.' She redoubled her efforts to get free.

'He already knows, miss.' The policeman's quiet words brought her struggles to an abrupt end.

'He—knows?' she whispered, and felt as if any moment now she would faint. Desperately she hung on to her swimming senses. 'He knows?' she repeated stupidly, and stared up at the blurred face beneath the blue peaked cap.

'He knows well enough, none better.' The older, stouter policeman, no sprinter, as he would be the first to admit, panted up beside his colleague.

'That's why they're using the *Sea Wind* to pull the vessel offshore, miss.' The younger policeman spoke gently, his eyes compassionate on Dee's tortured face. 'Mr Archer knows the risk, and so does George. It was they who suggested using the *Sea Wind* in the first place, because the tug's strong enough to pull the vessel off the beach without help. If the smaller tugs were used, the local ones, they'd have to use four or five of them for towing, and a lot more men,' he added significantly.

'This is a job for single men. . . .'

And she had accused him of taking on the job purely in order to win the salvage money, of robbing the local men of work that was rightfully theirs.

'Nat!'

She turned, still in the grip of the young policeman, and held out her arms towards Nat. Her hands encountered nothing but empty air, and tears coursed unchecked down her cheeks as she whispered despairingly,

'Nat!'

He could not have heard her from that distance. It was doubtful if even the policeman who held her caught her almost soundless cry. But something made Nat turn and look back towards her. For a brief, wonderful moment, hope flared within her, then it died again just as quickly. Nat did not take even one step back towards her. Instead he remained where he was, on the spot where he had turned, and just looked at her, it seemed for a long, long time. But her eyes were too blinded by tears to read what was in his look. Frantically she dashed a hand across them, seeking to clear her vision, so that she could read the message, if there was one for her, in his look. But the traitorous tears continued to flow, and even as she blinked them away Nat turned and walked on.

The sun glinted on his gold ear-ring as he turned, and she watched helplessly as his tall, upright figure grew smaller, going away from her across the empty sand, walking calmly, deliberately, towards the vessel that was a stranded bomb. And she would never know if there had been a message for her in his look or not.

CHAPTER ELEVEN

She got out of the police car and sat down on the sand dunes, and began a thousand years of waiting.

'There's a line coming out from the tug—look! He's missed it—no, he hasn't, it's landed. Mr Archer's got it, he's tying up. Here comes another. They must be going to use a double tow—I suppose one wouldn't be enough, it'd break.'

Nat had said the line broke in the storm the night before.

'That's both lines secured. Looks like they're going to tow the vessel out stern first, from the way he's tied her. Awkward, that.'

The young policeman kept up a running commentary, and Dee did not know whether to hope he would carry on talking, or wish he would be quiet. She could see for herself what was going on. Her eyes were clear enough now, she thought bitterly. Now it no longer mattered. In a way she wished she could not see so well. Her teeth clenched so tightly with the strain, she felt as if her jaw would crack. It was like watching a slow-motion film, she thought shudderingly, knowing everything that was happening— everything, she swallowed convulsively, everything that was likely to happen, but insulated from it all by a ghastly sense of unreality.

She ran the fine dune sand through her fingers, seeking to ease the crackling tension with movement. Gather up a handful, and let it dribble away again. Gather up another handful . . . and another. Feel the tiny grains slip away like the sand in an egg timer. Another handful. . . . It was like timing away the seconds of Nat's life. Timing away her own, because without Nat her life had no meaning.

Watching the precious minutes tick by inexorably, one by one, until the time came for high tide. Or the explosion. Which would come first?

'The vessel's afloat—look! She's beginning to lift herself, to move....'

The policeman felt the tension too, but to him it was an impersonal thing, part of his job. To her.... Dee concentrated on the vessel. On Nat. The ship *was* moving, she watched it carefully, counting the movement. Up, a pause, then down again. Up.... The movement would shake the spilled chemical, perhaps roll it nearer to the water coming through the holed side. Her nerveless fingers let the sand go and gripped one another instead. Her knuckles showed white with the force of her grip, but she did not notice. Her whole attention was riveted on the vessel, on Nat.

'Mr Archer's coming off her, look. He's jumping for it!'

Nat's figure outlined for a second against the sky as he quitted the foundered vessel with a mighty leap that took him far into the shallows. A shower of spray rose round him as he landed, but instead of wading ashore he turned instantly and walked out into deeper water, reaching for something Dee could not see. She rose to her feet the better to see, but the policeman spotted it first.

'He's got a rowboat there—look, just beyond the ship. He's managed to scramble in. My word, he's a good oarsman! He's setting up a cracking pace. I wish he was in our police rowing team.'

But no oarsman, however good, could hope to outdistance the blast, if the ship exploded now.

'He's almost at the tug. I wish I'd timed him, I reckon he's set up a record,' her companion said admiringly.

Fear was a fine goad to speed, and Nat feared for the town. Dee just feared....

'He's reached the tug, look. He's shinning up a rope. He's on deck!' It was like listening to a sports commentary on the radio, Dee thought desperately. The young policeman had missed his vocation. 'They've started the engine. They're pulling away....'

'Nat!'

Her hands flew to her lips and imprisoned her anguished cry. With fear wide eyes she stared at the *Sea Wind* as slowly, infinitely slowly, it gathered momentum and began to pull away from the shore. The twin hawsers joining the two ships rose out of the water, scattering bright drops as they came. It was like being on the fishing smack all over again, she thought numbly, waiting for the tow to snap tight. What would happen when it did? Would the resulting jerk be enough to set off the explosion?

'Nat! Oh, Nat....'

But this time he could not hear her, he could not turn back to look at her. He had to go on, and take his deadly charge along with him. The ropes snapped tight, and she caught a hard breath. A visible shudder went through the stricken vessel, but the tow held.

'Just look at that, now!' the policeman breathed admiringly.

Dee did not want to look. She longed to shut her eyes, to hide her face in her hands. It took every ounce of her strength to force herself to watch. Two figures were plainly visible on the tug—one large and bulky, that was George, the other tall and straight and slim, a black-clad silhouette, high up on the bridge.

'She's rising to the pull—look!'

The crippled vessel stirred, sluggish, but obedient to the ropes, buoyant now on the full tide. It still lay half on its side. Dee had seen fish float like that after being stunned by an underwater explosion set off deliberately by poachers. But this explosion had not happened yet; that was still to come. She sat down again, abruptly. She knew, with a dreadful sense of inevitability, that it *would* come. The only question was, when?

'If only he can tow it out of range of the town in time,' the policeman muttered tensely from beside her.

The *Sea Wind* would not be out of range. Nat and George—Dee tried hard to make herself remember that George was out there on the tug too—would be on the spot, only the length of the hawsers separated the tug from its deadly follower. She gripped her arms around her knees, hugging them tightly up to her chin, instinctively trying to hold on to something, anything, when all she longed to do was to put her arms around Nat.

The stricken vessel wallowed, half submerged, offering a resistance to its easy passage through the water that slowed the whole operation to a crawl. Dee longed to scream at the slowness of it all, longed for the moments to fly past, and be done with the waiting. Longed for them to go on for ever, because when the explosion came...

She gripped her fingers together, and they slipped apart again, her hands wet with the tension of waiting. She rubbed them in the sand to dry them, vaguely aware of a tinny sound starting up from somewhere behind her.

'That's the car radio.' The policeman ducked his head into the Panda car to answer the summons. Dee did not look round. Her eyes were glued to the *Sea Wind*, watching until they ached with the strain. She rubbed her hand across her eyes to clear them, and when she opened them again she could no longer see Nat. The slow progress of the boat was deceptive, the tug was now too far away for her to be able any longer to discern Nat's figure on the bridge.

'That was HQ on the radio.' The policeman returned to stand beside her. 'They said they reckon the tug's far enough out of the bay now for the danger from the blast to be minimal.' Formal words, repeating the radioed instruction. It did not minimise the danger to Nat.

'A few broken windows, that should be all.'

A few broken lives. Vaguely Dee wondered if George

was engaged. 'A job for single men,' Nat had said, so George could not be married.

'There might be a big wave pushed ashore when the vessel blows up, but there'll be no one on the beach while the tide's full, so it won't matter.'

So the policeman, too, knew it would blow up. He, too, felt the inevitability. Dee looked at him, dumbly. Viewed impartially, it probably did not matter all that much. Two lives against many.

'Sorry, miss, I didn't mean ... I didn't think.' He looked desperately uncomfortable. 'Can I give you a lift back into town?' He tried to plaster over his gaffe.

'No, you go on. I'll wait here.' Her voice came out flat, devoid of life. She did not say what she was waiting for—she had no need to. The reason for the waiting hung heavy between them.

'I'll stay on with you for a while, if you like,' the officer offered kindly. 'There's no need for me to go back straight away.'

'No, you carry on.' Dee did not add, 'I'd rather be alone.' Her eyes begged him for her, 'Please, go away. Go now, before....'

The officer looked down at her for a moment, then he nodded gravely, and Dee relaxed. He had read her message—read it, and understood. Had Nat read her message, when he turned and looked back at her across the sand? Had he understood? Or hadn't he cared? She would never know now.

'Well, if you're sure?' Fortunately the policeman did not argue, or try to persuade her. He climbed back into his car and she heard the radio stutter again, instructing him to go somewhere else, attend to someone else's needs. Perhaps to an accident, or a street disturbance, or just a kitten stuck up a tree. She heard him answer, his voice crisp, interested. He had already forgotten Nat and George and the tug, his mind tuned to his next call.

The Panda car started on its way. Dee did not see it go. She only heard the sound of the engine grow fainter, and die away, and wondered if the car had got sand in its carburettors during its long wait on the dunes. Then the sound disappeared, and there was only herself, and two small specks that were the ships, still faintly visible right on the horizon, and the soft sough of the wind to keep her company, the eternal wind that always blew across the dunes no matter how hot the day. It blew now, shifting the tiny grains of sand here and there, picking them up and dropping them down again somewhere else, much as she had done. Much as life was doing, with her, and with Nat. Soon she would be somewhere else, in the north, doing a job she no longer wanted, but doing it just the same, because there was nothing else left for her to do. Nothing left without Nat. . . .

The explosion brought her to her feet.

It was fainter than she thought it would be. Her dazed mind registered the fact, and wondered at it. Resented it, even. Her whole world erupted in a single tremendous holocaust, leaving her to pick up the pieces as best she might, and all that reached her ears was a dull, reverberating roar, that could have been a distant clap of thunder, but she knew it was not.

She clenched her hands until her nails dug ridges into her palms, but however hard she strained her eyes she could not see any sign of the tug. A dense pall of smoke mushroomed up from beyond the horizon, where the ships had disappeared it seemed only moments before, but of the two vessels there was no sign. Dee waited frozenly, staring out across the empty sea, staring out into her empty future. After a long time a high, rolling swell became visible, racing across the bay. It ran inshore, losing momentum as it came, and thumped against the sea wall with a loud slap, throwing up showers of spray. A flotilla of smaller waves followed it, then the water quietened again and resumed its regular rhythm, beginning to draw back from the beach at the behest of the receding tide.

And that was that....

Dee stirred and turned away, then started to walk, slowly, as if she was very old. She felt a hundred years old, only there would be no congratulatory telegram from the Palace. There was nothing to congratulate her about. Her legs felt wooden, and she stumbled, groping her way blindly, unaware of the direction she took. She seemed to walk for a long time, until a cottage loomed in front of her, and a garden gate that looked vaguely familiar. Just inside it, on the path, stood Hugh's wife, in a bright gingham apron. She held out her arms towards Dee and said,

'Come inside, my lamb. Come inside and have a drink of cocoa. You'll feel better when you've had a hot cup of cocoa.' It seemed to be her panacea for all ills, Dee thought numbly, but she went inside, and submitted meekly to the motherly little woman's ministrations, too exhausted to be capable of protest, to be capable of remaining on her feet for a moment longer.

The cocoa did help, in a way. It took away some of the frozen numbness that gripped her, and brought her half alive again. But coming alive brought back the pain....

'Where's Hugh?' She forced herself to ask about Hugh, ask about anything, to stop herself from thinking about Nat.

'He's taken the fishing smack and gone out to....' Hugh's wife checked herself hastily.

'He's gone out to the wreckage,' Dee finished the sentence for her. 'There may not be any there to find.' Frozenly she pointed out the obvious. She heard herself speak through a kind of dream, and add, 'No, I don't want any lunch, thanks.'

'We had ours a bit early, Hugh and I.'

Was it that time already? Nearly mid-afternoon?

'Yes, I'd love another cup of cocoa.'

Perhaps it would warm the ice inside her some more, melt it, and let the merciful tears flow. There might be some relief in tears.

'Hugh will be back by and by.' With the fishing skipper's wife, everything happened by and by. It could mean anything, from later, to any minute now. The thought stirred Dee into action.

'I feel a bit better, now.' She tried to smile her thanks, but the smile would not come. Her face felt as wooden as her legs. 'Thanks for the cocoa.' Banalities, but they helped to fill the empty space left by words that could not be spoken, questions that could not be asked. 'I'll go and collect my car, it's in the park behind the Town Hall.' How many lifetimes ago had she parked it there? Parked it, and then quarrelled with Nat.

'Hugh will go along with you, if you wait until he comes back.' Concern showed in the kindly eyes and the apple-cheeked face.

'No, I'll manage on my own.' She dared not wait to see Hugh, to hear what tidings he brought home with him. Knowing was bad enough. Having what she knew confirmed could only make it worse.

She tensed as a car came towards the cottage, then relaxed as it passed, and she saw that it was blue. Hugh's car was a bright red, the same colour red as her cotton skirt. Perhaps the fishing skipper was not back yet, maybe he had not even reached the harbour. So if she did not want to see Hugh, why was she walking in the direction of the harbour?

'The car park's near the sea front.' She tried to tell her feet it was near the sea front. Tried to force them to turn round, and go in the direction of the Town Hall, but like the red shoes in the fairy tale, they seemed to have a will of their own, outside her control. Panic rose in her as they carried on walking in the direction of the harbour. She longed to cry out, 'Take me back. Take me the other way.' But if they heard her urgent command, they ignored it, and helplessly Dee felt herself forced ever nearer to the quayside, ever closer to the empty space that had so recently held the *Sea Wind* at berth.

The empty space mocked her, cruelly final. The *Sea Wind* was not there, she knew it could not be there. It would never berth there, never berth anywhere, ever again.

A smart white cabin cruiser nosed through the assorted harbour craft, making its way towards the *Sea Wind*'s empty berth. Dee watched it with a stirring resentment. Even in such a short space of time, there was another boat eager to take over the *Sea Wind*'s place. No one would ever take Nat's place, with her....

She watched the cabin cruiser come closer. It was a large boat, capable of ocean travel, and it looked new. White paint gleamed in the sunshine, and everything about it shone. The tall, bulky figure on deck looked familiar. She knitted her brows, and her resentment deepened. It was George. He had not taken long to change his allegiances, either, she thought bitterly.

The new vessel slid into place neatly and without fuss, and George let down a plank over the side, just such a plank as he had let down from off the *Sea Wind*, narrow, and bouncy, and fearsome to walk along. He ran down it catfooted, trailing a rope with him, and started to tie it to a mooring ring before realisation dawned upon Dee that—George was with Nat, on the tug!

And now he was here, unharmed, on the quayside.

'*Nat!*'

George straightened from his task at her cry, and turned round, recognised her.

'Mr Archer's on the cruiser, miss. Didn't you know? He sent Hugh to tell you, to let you know....'

Dee did not stop to listen to any more. Her feet flew on wings along the quayside. They touched the plank and raced up it. She knew, now, why her feet had brought her here. She did not even look down, to see where they trod.

The plank bounced, but she did not care. As if by magic her feet carried her along the plank, unerringly to the deck, to where a tall, slim, black-clad figure was just emerging from below.

'Nat!'

He was alive. By some miracle, he had escaped the explosion, and *he was alive*.

'Nat!'

She sped along the deck, sobbing his name, disbelieving, wanting to believe, unable to grasp the wonderful, impossible reality that Nat was alive.

'I don't think the *Sea Wind* sustained any damage.' He turned and spoke to the man who had followed him up the companionway, a man with a fair, balding head, and wearing an office suit. 'The explosion came from under the water, fortunately the vessel was almost submerged by then, and the blast went away from the tug. That's why we towed it out stern first. But if you do find any damage, let me know, and I'll have it made good.'

'Indeed, Mr Archer, you will not,' his companion was adamant. 'The whole town owes you a debt of gratitude for what you did today.' He ignored Nat's deprecating gesture, and went on, 'if the *Sea Wind*'s been damaged at all, we'll have it repaired at our own expense. The price we offered you for the tug will stand. There's no more to be said.' He stopped Nat's protest with a raised hand, and Dee halted uncertainly as they both came towards her across the deck. She recognised Nat's companion. He was one of the partners from Wainwrights, the ship's brokers, and it sounded as if he had purchased the *Sea Wind* from Nat. Then what was he doing with Nat on the deck of the cruiser? She took a backward step, uncertain whether to go or to remain unwilling to intrude on a private business conversation, incapable of leaving Nat. Her movement caught the attention of the older man, and he nodded towards her with a kindly smile as he shook hands with Nat.

'I've got no more to say,' he repeated firmly, 'but I think perhaps your charming visitor might have.'

Dee had only four words that really mattered.

'Nat, I love you.'

She had spent the last few hours whispering them to herself, over and over again, wishing Nat had been there to whisper them to. And now he was here, standing in front of her, standing over her, looking down at her, and she could not say them. Her tongue stuck to the roof of her mouth, her throat felt as dry as the dune sand, and the words refused to come.

He did not help her. He did not speak to her, or move. He just stood there on the deck, tall and slim and straight, watching her. Waiting. Waiting for what? If only he would speak, give her some sign! His face was enigmatic, his eyes inscrutable. Dee tried to read the expression in his eyes, and had to turn her own away, unable to meet his look.

'I came . . . I came. . . .' Her voice dried up, unable to tell him why she came. How could she say to this tall, aloof, silent escapee from death, 'I came because I love you'?

'Yes?'

Just the one monosyllable, as unhelpful as the silence.

'I came. . . .' She gulped, and took her courage in both hands. It promptly oozed away like the dune sand through her fingers, and left her weak, and trembling. 'I came to p-pay you for the chocolates, and the c-cotton wool.' She stammered out the first words that came into her head, blurting them out in a rush. They sounded as silly as her excuse for coming into Penzyn through the storm, to buy cake.

'So you came to pay me.' He said it quietly, without inflection, and she could not tell whether it was a statement or a question.

'I couldn't let you start out on your trip without paying you.' It sounded even sillier, because she had no money with her. She could not let him go without telling him she loved him. . . .

'You're going away for two years.' She made it sound as if he could not afford to go unless he had the money for the chocolates and the cotton wool. 'I'm babbling,' she told herself, and stopped. 'Is this the cruiser you'll be using?' That sounded better. Calmer. Inspiration came to her aid, and told her the reason for the cruiser. Perhaps Nat would talk about his vessel? All seagoing men talked about their ships. 'Will George go with you?'

'No.'

'We're back where we started,' Dee thought hysterically, and stamped on the hysteria with desperate force. She dared not lose control now.

'It looks a roomy boat.' She gave him a lead. 'If he just says Yes, I'll scream!' she promised herself.

'Would you like to see over her?'

'Yes.'

She was doing the same thing now. The hysteria bubbled up again, very close to the surface. She felt like a cauldren with all her emotions rapidly coming to the boil under the lid. It took all her willpower to suppress them, but somehow she managed it, enough to make her capable of responding more or less sensibly when he added,

'This way. Mind the steps.'

It was like a house agent showing an interested client round a semi-detached. Urgently, Dee forced her whole attention on the steps. There were ten of them. She counted them carefully as she went down. One, two, three. . . . By the tenth, she had herself under control again.

'It's big.' The size of it took her by surprise. They came down into what looked like a living cabin. It was more than big enough for two, much too large for one. She made herself register the details of the furniture, the decorations. If she remembered them well enough, she would be able to visualise Nat among them....

'There's a sleeping cabin almost the same size.' He did not offer to show her the sleeping cabin.

'I'll have to go.' Suddenly she could not bear to remain there any longer. Could not endure being with Nat, because he did not love her. If he cared for her, he would have told her about his journey, helped her out of her difficulty now. She choked,

'I'll have to go.'

It meant going down the plank, alone. Fear caught at her at the thought of going down the plank, and she thrust it away to join the hysteria. Her feet had brought her here, and she would make them take her away again. Make them run away.

'You haven't paid me yet for the chocolates and the cotton wool.' Nat stood in front of her, between herself and the steps. She looked round desperately, but there was no other exit, only the door into the sleeping cabin. She looked away hastily, and back again at Nat, her eyes enormous in her white face.

'I've got no money with me.' He would have to let her go, to fetch the money to pay him. The burning light that lit his black eyes told her he would not....

'In that case I'll take my payment in kind, on the spot.' He used her own words to mock her.

Dee fought him.

She fought him with her fists and her feet. Her teeth were clenched too tightly to allow her to bite, otherwise she might have used those, too. At the first touch of his hands on her shoulders, all the pent-up fear and hysteria and love and hate that were a volatile mixture of her feelings for Nat erupted with an explosion that rivalled that of the wrecked vessel.

His head bent above her, his lips hovered close to her own. Frantically she twisted her head away. If he kissed her, she was lost. Despair added impetus to her struggles, and she fought as one possessed. Her breath came in harsh, panting gasps, and a mist danced in front of her eyes. Nat's lips brushed her forehead, her temple. They burned like a charge of high-voltage electricity, with a pain she could not bear. With every ounce of her reserve strength she gave a final convulsive struggle and twisted out of his arms, and with an inarticulate cry stumbled for the companionway. The sharp edge of the steps banged against her shin as she ran, but she clawed her way upwards, uncaring for the pain. She could hear Nat coming behind her, close behind her. He must not catch up with her. She had not the strength left to break his hold again. Blindly she fled across the deck towards the ship's rail, where the plank lay.

'You little fool! If you try to go down that on your own, you'll land in the dock! How you managed to come up it in the first place, goodness knows!'

She was actually on the plank when he grabbed her. He plucked her from off it with no more effort than if she had been a child.

'Dee, listen to me.' He shook her, stilling her struggles that were ineffective now because her strength was spent. 'I have to sail in a few days.'

'Sail where you want to, I don't care!' she shouted back at him hysterically, heedless now of betraying her feelings, blinded by the tears that ran in rivers down her cheeks. She was helpless to check them, she no longer tried, and they could not check the burning pain that the touch of his lips had left behind.

'You go your way, and I'll go mine,' she sobbed. 'Just let me go. . . .'

'I'll never let you go,' he ground out, and shook her again, roughly this time, forcing her to listen. 'Never, as long as I live, do you hear?' He shouted, to make sure she did.

She heard, and suddenly she went deathly still. Had she really heard aright, or was hearing him, seeing him, feeling him holding her, merely some sort of delirium her mind had conjured up to comfort her, when all the while she knew that Nat was dead?

'I'll never let you go. We belong to one another, Dee.'

It wasn't delirium. No fantasy could equal this.

'Our lives are tied together, the way the tides are tied to the moon. Nothing can alter it. Nothing can sever it.' His voice was quieter now, urgent, compelling, but it had in it the ring of steel. 'Go if you have to. I sail next week. But if you take your job in the north, maybe even marry someone else up there, you'll still belong to me. You'll always belong to me, for as long as we both live. You can't escape your destiny.'

She did not want to, so long as destiny gave her to Nat. He had put a line on the fishing smack, and a line on her life, and she gladly gave him the rest of it in payment for the salvage.

'I love you, Dee. I love you,' he groaned, and buried his face in her hair, straining her close to him with urgent arms. 'I've got to sail next week. I kept putting off the sailing date, hoping. . . .' He drew a hard, pained breath. 'I can't delay any longer now. Don't make me go without you.'

She knew, now, why he had not mentioned to her when he would sail. She knew, too, that he would sail without her if he had to. A woman's lot is to follow her man, but joyously she knew that Nat was her man. She belonged to him, and he to her, for ever.

'Sail with me, Dee, beyond the harbour bar,' he pleaded. 'I'll keep you safe.' He thought she was afraid, when all the time it was Nat who was her harbour, his arms her harbour bar. They tightened around her, fiercely pulling her to him, as if he was afraid she might break free even now, and fly away. 'Marry me,' he begged, and all the steel was gone.

Love was left.

It glowed through the passionate entreaty that lit the

depths of his black eyes, offering himself, imploring her. It lived in the ecstasy of his lips that covered her own, seeking, demanding. She raised her face to his so that they no longer had to seek, and they closed together in a lingering sweetness that answered his demand. With a long sigh she surrendered to his arms, and her own rose, her hands clasping tightly behind his head, embracing her destiny.

Their love was not born to rest upon quiet waters. Calmly, at last, Dee accepted what could not be altered. She knew there would be times when they would quarrel, times even when she might feel she hated Nat, but there would never be a time when she could live without him. Wild storms disturbed the surface of the sea, tempestuous, devastating, but underneath the storms the deeps remained steadfast. And always, even in storm, the sea was beautiful. Their love held the same indestructible beauty as the sea, the same steadfast depths.

'Marry me,' Nat begged her hoarsely.

'We'll quarrel. . . .'

'We'll always make it up.'

'I'll marry you,' she whispered, but it was loud enough for Nat to hear. She tilted her head back, her face luminous with her love, convincing him at last. 'I love you . . . I love you. . . .' Now she could say the words, now there was no barrier between them. Her lips sought his, hungry to show him her love. A long, sweet time passed between them, sealing their love.

'Come and see your future home.' He raised his head at last, reluctantly, his lips stealing one more kiss from her rosy face, and he smiled down at her, urging her to go with him. 'I bought the cruiser big enough for two, for both of us, hoping. . . .'

That must have been the day he went to the ship's brokers, the day she had bought her dress. They had both of them been hoping, and neither of them knew. She sighed, mourning the waste of time, then smiled back, suddenly gay.

'And all because you drove off with my suitcase that day. You knew it was in the back of your truck all the time,' she accused him.

'How else was I to get to know the girl I intended to marry?'

'You knew, even then?'

'I knew, even then,' Nat admitted seriously. 'And now you can pay me for the chocolates and the cotton wool.' Once more his lips exacted his payment in kind, then he took her hand and led her back down the companionway, to see over the vessel that he had bought to take him on his two-year journey round the world. The vessel that he had bought for them both.

The sleeping cabin was furnished like the living cabin, plainly but beautifully, without regard to cost. Furnished, Dee saw now with clearer sight, to provide a home fit for a bride. She crept closer under Nat's arm, trembling, but no longer afraid. The walls were unadorned, except for one thing. He turned her to look at it.

'I had to take your picture with me, because you had taken my heart. I couldn't leave them both behind.'

A strong man's voice broke at the thought of sailing away and leaving them behind. A brave man's courage, that set at nought what the policeman had described as a floating bomb, quailed at the agony of sailing without her. His eyes burned with remembered pain, and his lips sought the only balm capable of healing it.

'Don't . . . don't. . . .' Dee turned swiftly into his arms, unable to bear his agony. 'You won't need your picture now.' Gently she teased his eyes back to life again, his voice back to laughter. 'You can give it to your magazine.'

'I share my work with the world, but not my heart,' he rebuked her. 'I'll always need my picture, just as I'll always need you.' He held her close, gazing at the picture, beautifully mounted in a large oval silver frame, of a girl dancing barefoot on a shell sand beach, with her skirt held high in outstretched hands, the bright ribbons of her petticoat flying. 'I'll always need you.' He turned from the picture to the original, urgent for reassurance that she would need him, too.

'It's a home fit for a queen.' From her own new strength Dee calmed his fears, turned his thoughts to the future . . . their future.

'It'll serve us for the next two years,' Nat compromised, 'but after that we'll have to decide where we want to live permanently. A boat's fine for two of us, but it's no place to bring up a family.' Tenderly he drew her close. 'We'll need a home ashore for our children.' He made her happiness complete, and crowned it by adding, 'Though we'll keep the cruiser, for when we want to escape for a while, just the two of us.'

'Just the two of us,' Dee murmured softly. 'In the meantime, we've got the boat.' Her confidence waned, suddenly. 'And that awful plank!' she remembered, her eyes wide.

'I'm having a gangway with hand rails made specially for you,' he promised her. 'Wainwrights are to deliver it tomorrow. And in the meantime,' he lifted her gaily into his arms, 'I promise I won't drop you in the dock.'

'I won't sail with you if you do,' she threatened, and then contradicted herself instantly, 'Perhaps I will, after all. Two years' cruising sounds too tempting to miss,' she conceded, her eyes teasing, laughing up into his.

'Two years' honeymoon sounds even better,' Nat told her contentedly.

The Mills & Boon Rose is the Rose of Romance

Every month there are ten new titles to choose from — ten new stories about people falling in love, people you want to read about, people in exciting, far-away places. Choose Mills & Boon. It's your way of relaxing:

March's titles are:

GREGG BARRATT'S WOMAN *by Lilian Peake*
Why was that disagreeable Gregg Barratt so sure that what had happened to Cassandra was her sister Tanis's fault?

FLOODTIDE *by Kay Thorpe*
A stormy relationship rapidly grew between Dale Ryland and Jos Blakeman. What had Jos to give anyone but bitterness and distrust?

SAY HELLO TO YESTERDAY *by Sally Wentworth*
It had to be coincidence that Holly's husband Nick — whom she had not seen for seven years — was on this remote Greek island? Or was it?

BEYOND CONTROL *by Flora Kidd*
Kate was in love with her husband Sean Kierly, but what was the point of clinging to a man who so obviously didn't love her?

RETRIBUTION *by Charlotte Lamb*
Why had the sophisticated Simon Hilliard transferred his attentions from Laura's sister to Laura herself, who wasn't as capable as her sister of looking after herself?

A SECRET SORROW *by Karen van der Zee*
Could Faye Sherwood be sure that Kai Ellington's love would stand the test if and when she told him her tragic secret?

MASTER OF MAHIA *by Gloria Bevan*
Lee's problem was to get away from New Zealand and the dour Drew Hamilton. Or *was* that her real problem?

TUG OF WAR *by Sue Peters*
To Dee Lawrence's dismay and fury every time she met Nat Archer, he always got the better of her. Why didn't he just go away?

CAPTIVITY *by Margaret Pargeter*
Chase Marshall had offered marriage to Alex, simply because he thought she was suitable. Well, he could keep his offer!

TORMENTED LOVE *by Margaret Mayo*
Amie's uncle had hoped she would marry his heir Oliver Maxwell. But how could she marry a maddening man like that?

Mills & Boon
Best Seller Romances

The very best of Mills & Boon Romances
brought back for those of you who missed
them when they were first published.
In March
we bring back the following four
great romantic titles.

DANGEROUS RHAPSODY
by Anne Mather

Emma's job in the Bahamas was not as glamorous as it seemed
— for her employer, Damon Thorne, had known her before —
and as time went on she realised that he was bent on using her
to satisfy some strange and incomprehensible desire for
vengeance ...

THE NOBLE SAVAGE
by Violet Winspear

The rich, appallingly snobbish Mrs Amy du Mont would have
given almost anything to be admitted to the society of the
imposing Conde Estuardo Santigardas de Reyes. But it was
Mrs du Mont's quiet, shy little companion who interested the
Conde ...

TEMPORARY WIFE
by Roberta Leigh

Luke Adams was in love with his boss's wife, and it was
essential that their secret should remain a secret — so Luke
made a temporary marriage of convenience with Emily Lamb.
But Emily didn't know Luke's real reason for marrying her ...

MASTER OF THE HOUSE
by Lilian Peake

Alaric Stoddart was an arrogant and autocratic man, who had
little time for women except as playthings. 'All women are the
same,' he told Petra. 'They're after two things and two things
only — money and marriage, in that order.' Could Petra prove
him wrong?

If you have difficulty in obtaining any of these books through
your local paperback retailer, write to:
Mills & Boon Reader Service
P.O. Box 236, Thornton Road, Croydon, Surrey, CR9 3RU.

The Mills & Boon Rose is the Rose of Romance

THE STORM EAGLE by *Lucy Gillen*
In other circumstances Chiara would have married Campbell Roberts. But he had not consulted her. And now wild horses wouldn't make her accept him!

SECOND-BEST BRIDE by *Margaret Rome*
Angie would never have guessed how the tragedy that had befallen Terzan Helios would affect her own life...

WOLF AT THE DOOR by *Victoria Gordon*
Someone had to win the battle of wills between Kelly Barnes and her boss Grey Scofield, in their Rocky Mountains camp...

THE LIGHT WITHIN by *Yvonne Whittal*
Now that Roxy might recover her sight, the misunderstanding between her and Marcus Fleming seemed too great for anything to bridge it...

SHADOW DANCE by *Margaret Way*
If only her new job assignment had helped Alix to sort out the troubled situation between herself and her boss Carl Danning!

SO LONG A WINTER by *Jane Donnelly*
'You'll always be too young and I'll always be too old,' Matt Hanlon had told Angela five years ago. Was the situation any different now?

NOT ONCE BUT TWICE by *Betty Neels*
Christina had fallen in love at first sight with Professor Adam ter Brandt. But hadn't she overestimated his interest in her?

MASTER OF SHADOWS by *Susanna Firth*
The drama critic Max Anderson had wrecked Vanessa's acting career with one vicious notice, and then Vanessa became his secretary...

THE TRAVELLING KIND by *Janet Dailey*
Charley Collins knew that she must not get emotionally involved with Shad Russell. But that was easier said than done...

ZULU MOON by *Gwen Westwood*
In order to recover from a traumatic experience Julie went to Zululand, and once again fell in love with a man who was committed elsewhere...

If you have difficulty in obtaining any of these books from your local paperback retailer, write to:

Mills & Boon Reader Service
P.O. Box 236, Thornton Road, Croydon, Surrey, CR9 3RU.
Available April 1981

SAVE TIME, TROUBLE & MONEY!
By joining the exciting NEW...

Mills & Boon Romance CLUB

WITH all these EXCLUSIVE BENEFITS for every member

NOTHING TO PAY! MEMBERSHIP IS FREE TO REGULAR READERS!

IMAGINE the *pleasure* and *security* of having ALL your favourite *Mills & Boon* romantic fiction delivered right to *your* home, absolutely POST FREE... straight off the press! No waiting! No more disappointments! All this PLUS all the latest news of *new books* and *top-selling authors* in your own monthly MAGAZINE... PLUS *regular* big CASH SAVINGS... PLUS lots of wonderful strictly-limited, *members-only* SPECIAL OFFERS! All these exclusive benefits can be yours – right NOW – simply by joining the exciting NEW *Mills & Boon* ROMANCE CLUB. Complete and post the coupon below for FREE full-colour leaflet. It costs nothing. HURRY!

No obligation to join unless you wish!

FREE CLUB MAGAZINE Packed with *advance news of latest titles and authors*

Exciting offers of FREE BOOKS For club members ONLY

Lots of fabulous BARGAIN OFFERS –many at **BIG CASH SAVINGS**

FREE FULL-COLOUR LEAFLET!
CUT OUT CUT OUT COUPON BELOW AND POST IT TODAY!

To: **MILLS & BOON READER SERVICE, P.O. Box No 236, Thornton Road, Croydon, Surrey CR9 3RU, England.**
WITHOUT OBLIGATION to join, please send me FREE details of the exciting NEW **Mills & Boon** ROMANCE CLUB and of all the exclusive benefits of membership.

Please write in BLOCK LETTERS below

NAME (Mrs/Miss) ....

ADDRESS ....

CITY/TOWN ....

COUNTY/COUNTRY .... POST/ZIP CODE ....

Readers in South Africa and Zimbabwe please write to:
P.O. BOX 1872, Johannesburg, 2000. S. Africa